C000089914

Kristina Beck

Passions and Peonies

Passions and Peonies

Copyright © 2020 Kristina Beck

All rights reserved. No part of this publication may be reproduced,
distributed, or transmitted in any form or by any means, including
photocopying, recording, or other electronic or mechanical methods,
without the prior written permission of the publisher, except in the
case of brief quotations embodied in critical reviews and certain
other noncommercial uses permitted by copyright law.

This is a work of fiction. Names, characters, places, and incidents
either are the products of the author's imagination or are used
fictitiously. Any resemblance to actual persons, living or dead,
businesses, companies, events, or locales is entirely coincidental.

ISBN-13: 978-3-947985-10-4

To Brady and Julia

1

LACEY

"No, Sky!" I stop short and yank my suitcase to my side. "You'd better be joking!"

An older man bumps into my shoulder. "Get out of the way, missy," he grumbles. I turn away from him, then move to the side of the walkway to avoid the bustling crowd.

"But why is your flight delayed? The blizzard isn't supposed to hit until tonight." I drop my backpack on top of my suitcase and press the phone to my ear. It's loud in here.

"It has nothing to do with the storm," Skylar explains calmly. "Supposedly, there's a technical problem. They don't know how long it'll take to fix or to get another plane. I'm on my way to check if I can get on another flight." *Ugh!* Nothing bothers her. She's a go-with-the-flow kind of gal. I usually am too, but not recently.

"You're never gonna get to JFK in time. You'll miss our flight to St. Thomas." I close my eyes and pinch the bridge of my nose. Like I need this shit right now.

"Don't worry about me. We don't want to lose our hotel room. Take the flight and I'll meet you at the hotel sometime today or, worst comes to worst, tomorrow. I'll find another connection or maybe find a direct flight."

Skylar is my stepsister, and she's as single as a Pringle as I am. She lives in Boston near my dad and stepmother. I didn't really want to meet her when my dad mentioned that he was serious with a woman who had a daughter my age. I was ready to hate her when I met her, but instead we clicked instantly. We've been great friends ever since.

She was supposed to take a flight to JFK so we could fly together to St. Thomas. What a kick in the ass. Why our trip?

"This is such bullshit. I knew you should've flown here last night or taken the train."

"You need to chill. I can feel you twitching through the phone. I know how badly you want to get out of New York City." I can practically see her rolling her eyes. "Your signature peppiness better show up by the time I arrive." I hear shuffling on the other end. "Lace, hold on a second."

"Okay." I squeeze my lower lip between my fingers.

What a funk I'm in. It's the second week in April, and a snowstorm is headed our way. It's spring, for crying out loud! The last time I saw snow in April was when I was little. I don't mind winter so much in

December, but once the holidays are over, I'm done. This year, I think it's snowed every day since Christmas, and I am so over it! Nothing fun happens, and I end up staying inside and hibernating. Hot, sunny weather is what I live for. I always have.

When Skylar called me in January, saying that she had seen a good deal for a week at an all-inclusive resort in St. Thomas, she didn't have to say much to convince me. We checked out airfare and booked everything that day. I've had a countdown on my calendar ever since.

My brother, Drew, and his fiancée, Sophia, got engaged last week… four months after they met. They're made for each other and are ridiculously happy. But I'm surrounded by couples who just got married or engaged. I've been to six weddings in the last twelve months. So of course, everyone is asking me when I'm going to meet my future husband. How the hell should I know? It's not like I have a crystal ball. I'm not even sure I want to get married.

It's not only the brutal weather and all those happy couples. I'm at a point in my life where I'm asking myself, is this really it? I go to work every day, to a job I happen to love. My sister-in-law, Jocelyn, is a dress designer, and I'm one of her assistants. I get to work with family and my schedule is flexible. I have a cute apartment in New York City. I'm very lucky, but I'm bored. Is this what I'll do day in and day out for the rest of my life?

I didn't think I'd stay here. A little dream of mine was to live somewhere that's warm all year round.

Maybe with a beach nearby. I was planning to go to college in Florida, but then my parents announced unexpectedly that they were getting a divorce. It hit me and my two brothers hard, so I decided to go to school in the city to stay close to them. But now, I need a break from all this cold, stormy weather and crazy love stuff to sort out my head.

"Okay. I'm back," she says. "I'm standing in a long line now waiting to talk to someone."

"Sky, we've had this trip planned since January. This fucking better not be a sign that this vacation is going to suck." I want to stomp my foot like a four-year-old.

"Everything happens for a reason, Lace. Enjoy getting out of the city. Don't forget—while it's snowing here, we'll be sitting by the pool soaking up the sun. Just try to look at the positive side."

"I usually do, but this just sucks." An announcement over the loudspeaker interrupts, and I realize I need to get moving. "Anyway… I know you're right. Hey, I'm about to get on the AirTrain. I'll probably lose connection at some point. Go get an update and keep me posted."

"Will do. I'll see you soon."

"Ciao."

I end the call and stuff my phone into my backpack. The train doors open, and I squeeze myself and my small suitcase into the crowded space. I didn't bring much with me… bikinis, shoes, a couple of cute outfits, and a lot of sunscreen. I wouldn't even care if my suitcase got lost. I have a change of clothes in my backpack.

I cross my fingers in hopes that everything will run smoothly. I'm sure, as soon as my plane takes off, my usual smile will magically reappear.

I hope!

2

WILL

"We're on standby, so let's hope we get lucky. If only one seat becomes free, you can take it. You need to get out of here," Josh says as we find seats in an empty row by the gate.

I can only nod at this point. Lack of sleep has hit me hard. I'm so tired, I'm at the point that I almost *can't* sleep. But—my best friend, Sawyer, needed me more this week than I needed to sleep. I feel like shit leaving him in the emotional state he was in, but Josh and I have to get back to work. Really, what Sawyer needs is a diversion from what happened a couple weeks ago. I wish he could've come with us. All I know is that I never want to be in his position. In the blink of an eye, he lost the love of his life. It reminds me of what my dad went through years ago.

Josh bumps my elbow. "Hey, I think you got lucky. They just called your name. Let's go see. And take your damn sunglasses off."

I grab my carry-on and follow him to the flight

attendant behind the counter. A few minutes later, I've got my sunglasses back on and I'm searching for my seat on the plane. I feel bad that Josh didn't get a seat, but he's on standby for the next flight.

It takes me forever to get to my row, because everyone's stuffing their giant bags into the overhead compartments. There'd better be space for mine. I zone in on the only empty seat ahead of me. Almost there. I approach the row and check the overheads nearby. Good—just enough room for my bag, one row back.

I check the seat to make sure it's mine. A young woman sits next to the window, leaning her head on her hand. Her baseball cap is dipped low, hiding most of her face. A tablet rests on her lap. I recognize the long, pink-striped, blond hair that's flowing over one shoulder. She was the one I saw waiting in line to board the plane. I couldn't see her face then, either, but for some reason, I couldn't stop watching her. And now I'll be sitting next to her during this flight.

She's wearing a Boston Red Sox cap and a New York Yankee hoodie. Who does that? Someone who's looking for trouble. I shake my head and settle in next to her.

Half an hour later, and she hasn't stirred once. I've tried to sleep but it didn't happen. The flight attendant stops at our row and secures his jiggling cart, then asks what I'd like to drink. The woman next to me sits up, stretches, and adjusts her cap. I try to stay focused on the attendant and tell him what I'd like.

"Here's your screwdriver, sir." He places a napkin on my tray and then the plastic cup on top of it. So much for saving the turtles. He asks my neighbor what she wants.

I won't look at her, but I don't know why. No, I do. Her lips were a glossy, petal pink and slightly parted when I first saw her. Sexy and kissable. I'm afraid to see the rest of her face. There's a vibe coming from her that feels... pleasurably weird. I can't explain it. Maybe that's why I couldn't stop watching her at the gate.

"I'll have a bloody mary, please." *I'll just peek.*

She puts her tray down, removes her cap, and ruffles her hair. A cloud of perfume wafts my way. I close my eyes and enjoy the way it teases my senses. It reminds me of my sister's flower shop when she gets a batch of fresh flowers. *I should've ordered two screwdrivers.*

"Thank you," she says as the attendant hands her the drink. Gingerly, she takes a sip. "Ahhh. Welcome to vacation. I couldn't get out of New York fast enough." I want to laugh, but I'm not sure if she's talking to me or to him.

We pay the attendant. She takes another sip, then picks up her tablet and places it on the tray next to her drink. At least she has something to occupy herself with. My phone decided to die permanently this morning, so I can't even listen to music or watch a movie. I rest my head against the back of the seat and try not to focus on her every movement.

I usually ignore the people I sit next to on a plane, but she's different.

The attendant comes around again, offering food, which we both decline. But when he approaches us later, offering more beverages, we order the same drinks as before. Now she turns off her tablet and starts talking.

"My friend was supposed to be in your seat, but her connecting flight was canceled," she says, turning my way. I hesitate and place my cup back on the tray. Then I finally take the plunge and look straight at her. My chest expands like my heart grew two sizes bigger, and my mouth goes dry. *I need to get off this plane. She's too gorgeous for my own good.*

Her beauty is so unexpected but familiar in some way. Like I know her... but I know for sure that I don't. I'd remember someone as stunning as she is. My eyes trace her perfect, glowing face. I'm glad I still have my sunglasses on because I'd probably look like an idiot, the way I'm staring at her.

"Cat got your tongue? Maybe you need to drink the rest of your drink to relax a little. Your jawline is so tight, and your sunglasses make you look so intense."

"Maybe." It's all that comes out of my mouth. I take a large gulp of my drink. She does the same with hers.

"I was in such a pissy mood when I got to the airport this morning, but as soon as I was on this plane, *bam*, it dissipated. Not too long from now, I'll be soaking up the sun with a frosty beverage in my hand. How could I not be happy?" Her enthusiasm is trying

9

to jump over the armrest onto my lap. I lean away from her.

"What about your friend?" *Why am I talking to her?*

"She got a connecting flight in Atlanta. She'll arrive a few hours after me. I'm so relieved that she found something before the storm rolled in."

I nod and drink again. We sit in pleasant silence, but I'm keenly aware of her movements. And she moves a lot. Maybe she's not just giddy. Maybe nervous?

"*Scheisse*," she yelps when the plane hits a patch of turbulence. Her bloody mary splashes onto her hand and down her sweatshirt. "Now I'm going to smell like tomato juice. Yuck. Typical me."

"You always smell like tomato juice?" I tease. "Or you always spill things?"

She arches an eyebrow. "Oh. I see. You have a sense of humor hidden behind your sketchy Ray-Bans."

"What does Scheisse mean?" I hand her my napkin. She grabs it out of my hand and combines it with hers. Neither are very effective.

"It means 'shit' in German. My brother's fiancée is from Germany. The first words I asked her to teach me were swear words, and I liked that one the best. It kinda stuck with me," she explains while rubbing the spot vigorously. "I need to go to the bathroom to rinse this out and change. Maybe you shouldn't sit next to me. I'm known to be a bit clumsy." She swigs the rest of her drink, puts the empty cup in mine, and secures her tray.

"I'll take the chance. Just stick with water from now on." I waggle my eyebrows at her, and she giggles.

She pulls her backpack from under the seat in front of her, attaches her cap to it, then stands up. She surveys the area around us. "I'm in the clear. No carts blocking the aisle, and it looks like the bathroom is empty."

I stand up and move into the middle aisle to let her out. I tower over her. The top of her head barely reaches my chin. For someone with such a strong personality, I thought she'd be taller.

"Don't miss me while I'm gone." She flashes me a smile that's brighter than the sun reflecting off the ocean, then walks down the aisle.

I slide back into my seat but lean over the armrest to watch her walk away. I try not to laugh when a strap from her backpack catches on the corner of a seat and yanks her backward. I'm not sure how that happened.

She chuckles, says something to the person who's in the seat, then continues to the bathroom. Turbulence shakes the plane suddenly, and she bangs into the bathroom door. I sit up to see if she's all right. She shakes her head and hurries inside.

Who is this girl?

"This is your captain speaking. We will be flying through a patch of rough turbulence during the next twenty to thirty minutes. Please return to your seats and fasten your seatbelts. During this time, please do not use the bathrooms. I will let you know once we're in the clear."

I fasten my seatbelt and look for her. An attendant knocks vigorously on the bathroom door where she is. Other attendants rush through the aisle, taking away any beverages or garbage. The plane shakes again. A couple of passengers yelp. I look toward the back of the plane and realize the attendants are buckling up too. That's when you know it'll be bad.

Turbulence doesn't scare me. I've flown so many times up and down the East Coast. There's always some kind of turbulence. I don't get motion sickness either.

Here she comes. She rushes down the aisle toward our row, holding onto the seats as she passes. Her face is flushed, and she's out of breath. Her new outfit consists of frayed jean shorts and a tight light-pink tank top that emphasizes her chest. It also matches the color of her lips. An attendant demands she sit down immediately.

"I've never changed clothes so fast in such a cramped space. What a fiasco! I'll probably have bruises tomorrow."

I don't have time to enjoy the view or even to get up, because, just as she tosses her backpack across me to her seat, she loses her balance and falls on top of me.

"*Ooph.* I'm so sorry." Other passengers laugh. "Well, maybe not." Her voice trails off.

Her face is a few inches away, and her enticing lips are dangerously close. I can feel her pounding heart as if it's introducing itself to mine. I wrap my arms around her narrow waist like they're her seatbelt. It feels like I've held her before. This comfort level, this instant connection, is bizarre, but I don't try to fight it. She doesn't try to move either, and I'm sure we look ridiculous with her legs stretched out into the aisle.

It's not her mouth that smiles, it's her eyes. The color draws me in. They're light yellow around the pupil, then turn into a pale green, and then gradually to a bluish green. They're amazing... and probably even more beautiful in the sunlight.

"In the arms of a gorgeous guy and on vacation. What else could a girl want? I'm glad I'm sucking on a mint." *Sucking* is not the word I want to hear when she's on top of me. "I'd offer you one, but the few I had left are up there on the bathroom floor. Damn turbulence." She babbles nervously. I think I'm getting to her too.

"Are you always this talka—? What's your name anyway?" Damn, I can't stop looking at her mouth. Can she see my eyes through the dark lenses?

"Are you always so mellow, Mr. Ray-Ban?"

Mellow? She should hear what's going on in my head. She traces her finger along my jaw. *Definitely not mellow.*

"I asked you a question first."

Her eyes narrow.

"Lacey Devlin and yep." She grins and tickles my side with one hand. The attendant yells at her again to sit down, so I let her go.

It's better that she's in her seat. All that wiggling

didn't help what was happening in my jeans. I hope she didn't feel it.

Sniff. Sniff. What happened to her perfume?

"If you smell disinfectant, it's me. I don't leave home without it. Especially when I fly. Want some?" She opens the front pocket of her backpack and pulls out a bottle.

I straighten in my seat and laugh. "Maybe later." If she's this entertaining in a plane, I can't imagine her on a normal day.

Once she's secured in her seat again, she shivers. "I wonder if I can get a blanket. I didn't think to bring another sweatshirt. I didn't bring a real coat—I went straight from the taxi to the train to the airport. But I guess it was stupid to only have a tank top and shorts in my backpack."

"I don't think you're going to get anything until the turbulence is over." Before I can talk myself out of it, I unzip my sweatshirt and take it off. "Here, put this on. You need it more than I do."

"Oh my gosh. You are so damn sweet. Are you sure? I'll give it back when I warm up."

"Sure. It's better than that Yankee one you were wearing." I smirk. "You don't look like a girl who wants to start a fight."

"I can't help it if I like both teams. I live in New York City, and my father lives in Boston."

The long sleeves get tangled when she slips her arms into them. "It's so soft inside!" She sniffs the material before she zips it up. "Mmm, and it smells good too. You're the best. Thank you."

"You're welcome. I went to Boston University with a baseball scholarship. I didn't get a chance to make it to the big leagues. But now you know why my sweatshirt says Boston Red Sox."

"What happened?"

"I had to choose between my family and baseball. Baseball lost. I still love to play, but it wasn't my only passion anyway."

At some point while I was talking, she snuggled up against me like she's warming up in front of a fire.

On a normal day, I would never in hell let a passenger lean against me or touch me in any way—but again, she's different. Obviously, she was just lying across my lap and I didn't mind at all. But Lacey has an innocence about her. It's her personality that's tempting me. She's so natural and easygoing.

She'll be a nice distraction for the rest of the flight, so I won't have to think about what I just left back in New York.

The flight gets bumpier. Things shift overhead, making me worry the compartments will burst open and suitcases will come flying out. An older woman across the aisle is mumbling something to herself and gripping the armrests. The passenger behind her is an interesting shade of green and is holding a barf bag.

When the plane dips again, Lacey's cold hand latches onto my forearm. Her eyes are squeezed shut, and she's biting her lower lip.

"Man, your hand is freezing." I lift up the armrest between us. "Give me your hands." Without opening her eyes, she extends her arms toward me. I envelop both hands in mine to warm them up. They are as soft as pussy willows.

I have literally lost my mind.

"Are you scared?" I squeeze her hands gently.

She opens her eyes and takes a deep breath. "I'm sorry. This turbulence is the worst. I'm trying to stay calm, but that was a rough dip. *Whoo.*"

"Do you feel sick?"

She shakes her head, glances at our hands, then at me. One side of her mouth rises. "I haven't had motion sickness of any kind before. I could be on a boat in the middle of a hurricane, and I'd still not get sick."

She's too good to be true.

Now that there's no barrier between us, she scoots a little closer to me. "Can you talk to me so I'll think about something else?"

"Like what?"

I twist in my seat to see her better. She does the same. Our faces are as close as before. "Like your name for starters. I feel kind of strange not knowing it when I'm wearing your sweatshirt, I'm stuck to your side, and your big, warm hands are holding mine."

That's a cue for me to let her hands go and to move back, but I don't. Because I don't want to. Her hands aren't even that cold anymore.

"I'm Will Mayes."

"Nice name. Now, tell me why you're wearing sunglasses. It's not bright in here." She takes a sharp breath. "Please tell me you're not a drug addict or something."

I burst out laughing because I've never taken drugs. "No, I just haven't slept in a long time. My eyes are dry."

"Aww, come on." She nudges my arm. "Take the sunglasses off. I already like what I see, but I'm dying to see your eyes. Show me the full picture."

3

LACEY

W ill hesitates but takes his hands from mine, then removes his sunglasses. He hooks them on the collar of his black T-shirt. Then his free hand finds its way back to mine and captures it once more. Isn't he full of surprises?

When our eyes lock, I'm spellbound. *Wow, wow, wow.* They do look tired, almost like he might have been crying, but that doesn't make them any less stunning. They're a bright gray green with long, thick brown eyelashes. His right eye has the most unusual golden specks in it, almost like someone placed them there to make a fashion statement. Perfect little squares that overlap as if part of a confetti mix.

And it's not just his eyes that are amazing. When I fell on him, he felt like complete muscle. The tight T-shirt he's wearing and the golden tan he's sporting… my imagination is running wild. His thick hair is light brown with blond streaks running through it, pushed back with some gel.

Now let's talk about his perfect lips—which happen to be one of my favorite parts of a man's body. The lower one is slightly bigger than the upper. They're a shade of medium pink and smooth like a newborn's skin. Maybe he uses a lot of lip balm. To have just one nip before this plane lands would make my day. If our faces get any closer, I might not resist the temptation. This magnetic pull is unbelievable.

These thoughts are not normal. Why am I so comfortable with a complete stranger? It's as if we've known each other from another lifetime. My hormones are in a frenzy just from sitting next to him —well, and *on* him. Why did we have to meet on a plane? Why not in a cute little café in New York? Once we land, we won't see each other again. I can fantasize, though. I'll enjoy him while I can. I'm up for doing something crazy.

"Those golden specks in your right eye are so beautiful."

"Thanks." A sweet grin forms on his face, and he rests the side of his head on the back of the seat, making him even more adorable.

"So, it's your turn to answer. Are you always this mellow or nice to strange women?"

"Which one should I answer first?"

"Mellow?"

He shakes his head, then looks away. A tiny birthmark sits sweetly just below the back of his left ear. "It's been a rough couple of weeks. Mix that with exhaustion and this is who you get. I'm a pretty laid-back kinda guy, but I'm usually in a good mood."

"Wanna talk about it?" I rub his upper arm with the back of one of my freshly manicured hands. "It might help to talk to a stranger."

"Not really. I'm tired of talking about it. It's not going to change what happened. But you're giving me the perfect distraction, so please don't stop."

"So that's why you're being so nice to me."

His mouth quirks at the corners. "I won't argue there. I thought I'd be miserable this entire flight. Or annoyed that someone would be talking my ear off. But you're the best cure for a bad mood. My friends and family tried before I left New York, but it didn't work. With you, it's easy. Can I put you in my pocket and take you home for whenever I need a pick-me-up?"

That's the sweetest thing I've ever heard, and my heart does a little dance.

"I'm not sure I'll fit," I flirt. I'd gladly let him keep me for future use. What can I say? I like to make people happy. I want to press him for more details, but he doesn't have to tell me anything.

"Well, then… I'll have to find another way to keep you around." He squeezes my hand again, reminding me that he's still holding it.

"I have an idea." I pull my hand away and sift through my backpack for my phone. "Let's take a selfie together. Then when you're crabby, you can look at the photo and remember how bizarre this flight was."

"I hate being in pictures, but I'll do it just for you."

I snuggle up to him again and lean my head against his, almost cheek to cheek. He takes my phone and extends it in front of us. His long, muscular arm gives us a better angle.

"Say beaches," he mutters. We both laugh after we say it. He takes several shots and gives me the phone back. We check out the pictures and delete the hideous ones. To be honest, we'd make an amazing couple. He has a beautiful smile. I hope it was a real one.

He points at a specific shot. "I want that one. Can I have your phone for a sec?"

"But I'm the only one in the picture!" My cheeks burn from embarrassment.

Before I know it, he enters his contact info. Only his first name and number. I'm surprised he gives it to me at all. Does that mean he wants to stay in touch?

He hands the phone back to me. "Do you use WhatsApp?"

I nod.

"Please send me the picture once you have a connection."

I crinkle my eyebrows. "Why do you want one only of me? I loved the other one when we were both looking in the same direction."

"Because you look the most beautiful in that one. Now, every time I see your bright face, it'll make things better."

I lean away. "Is your phone full of pictures you take with girls on planes?" I'm trying to be funny, but that'd be really shitty if he does this all the time.

Pretending to be sad when he really isn't. He'll probably try to steal my passport or phone. Or maybe use my photo on dating sites. My stomach clenches.

"Hell, no. I told you I don't like pictures. And I try to avoid talking to the people who sit next to me. I put my AirPods in and block out everything and everyone. Except this time, my phone died, so that wasn't possible."

"Should I leave you alone then?" I stiffen.

He takes hold of my hand again and pulls me closer. "You stay right here." My shoulders relax as my heart melts a little bit more.

"I feel bad saying this, but I'm glad my friend missed her flight. I wouldn't have met you if she hadn't." I bite my lip. He doesn't respond, but I don't want him to because he's staring at my lips like he wants to devour them. I wish he would. I'm tingling from head to toe, and my belly swirls with excitement. I can't wait to tell Sky. She'll never believe it.

The plane dips again, pushing us closer together.

"I'm glad too." His eyes dilate, and his breathing increases. He leans in and I take his face in my hands. My lips brush his like a feather, but we break apart when an attendant announces on the intercom that we're descending.

We gaze at each other, both knowing that the opportunity has passed us by. It's probably for the best —I have a feeling that one kiss from him would lead to a lot more, and it wouldn't be enough.

Another announcement distracts us, and we pretend

to clean up our area. There's no mess, but we have to—or at least *I* have to occupy myself. We aren't holding hands anymore but our arms touch. I've changed my mind about telling Sky or anyone about Will. I want this only for myself. I'll keep the sweet memories of him tucked close to my heart for a rainy day.

The plane touches down. We're far enough back that it will take us a while to get off the plane. I stare at his tight muscles as he removes his carry-on from overhead. If timing and location were different, I wouldn't let him get away. That's what I'd tell my friends to do if they were in the same position.

Finally the line is moving, and Will lets me go ahead of him. As we get closer to the exit, I start to panic. What should I say to him when we have to part? What if he just walks away without saying goodbye?

He's still behind me as we approach the terminal. I can feel him watching me. His gaze tickles my entire body like a feather. We get separated once we get to customs, but every time I look in his direction, he's watching me. He doesn't even try to look away. I do, though, because his facial expression concerns me. His eyebrows are stuck together, and his jawline is tight like before. It's as if he's at war with himself.

It's a long wait, but I finally get through customs. I search for Will, but I don't see him anymore. My stomach turns and nausea sets in. *That's it. It's over.* I'll never see him again. My chest feels heavy, and I almost feel like I'm going to cry.

Just as I turn the corner, someone pulls me aside. I screech.

Will!

"I couldn't walk away without doing this."

My mouth opens to respond, but he silences me with his lips. They're exactly how I imagined them. Soft, gentle, perfect. He wraps one arm around my lower back and cups my cheek with the other. His tongue seduces my lips, and I open for him without hesitation. All the chaos around us disappears. It's only me and him.

Our kiss comes to an end, and we gaze silently at each other for a moment. Then the hunger that was in his eyes on the plane takes over, and I match it with my own. My backpack slides off my arm as I rise onto my toes and grab his shirt, pulling him to me. I capture his lips this time. We wrap our arms around each other and fall deeper into the heated kiss.

This is only supposed to be a goodbye kiss, but it feels like so much more. He pulls away, and I already feel empty. His thumb caresses my cheek. "I won't forget you." He pecks my lips one more time and walks away.

My feet are glued to the ground. I can hardly breathe. He's stolen my breath and my heart. I trace my tingling lips with my finger and find myself smiling. That kiss won't last a lifetime, but the memory of it—of him—will. How could any other man compare to that?

4

LACEY

The sign for baggage claim grabs my attention. I'm still searching for Will, but he's nowhere in sight. I don't know if I'm sad or relieved. No, I'm not relieved—far from it. I'm crushed, but I can't stop smiling either. Nothing like this has ever happened to me before. I've had a couple of serious relationships, but the connections were never instant or so intense.

Is this how Drew felt when he met Sophia for the first time? I shake my head. No, it's not the same. They're engaged to be married. I met Will on a plane. I said I wanted a little excitement in my life, and I got it when least expected.

That's. All. It. Was.

Beads of sweat form on my forehead as I wait for the transfer bus. It's hot as hell out here. Why am I still wearing my sweatshirt? I guess he took my brain with him too. I lift the bottom to remove it but stop midway. It smells like Will… because it *is* Will's. Oh no! Did he let me keep it, or did he forget I had it? I unzip and take it off, then I look around to see if anyone's watching me. In the clear. I put the sweat-shirt to my nose and inhale. It's a mix of fabric soft-ener and sandalwood. It's him. *Perfect.* When I wrap it around my waist, something falls out of a pocket and rolls away. I pick it up and laugh—it's a 30 SPF lip balm. I knew it! I shove it back in the pocket.

The hotel shuttle bus stops near me and blows a nice plume of exhaust in my face. *Climate control, people!* I secure my suitcase, then find a seat. The air condi-tioning is a dream. My phone had no connection in the airport, so let's see if it does now. It does! I melt into my seat as I sift through the selfies we took together. Hands down, he's the most gorgeous guy I've ever met. I open WhatsApp, create a new post, and attach the photo. My finger lingers over Will's name. Should I send it to him?

What if he responds? *But what if he doesn't?* They always say you should wait twenty-four hours before you make a decision when you're conflicted. But maybe I should just let the nice memory of today be enough. Why take the chance of ruining it? I hope I'm not saying all these things out loud.

I close WhatsApp and shut my eyes. I'll be at the hotel soon, and Sky will be here in a couple of hours. First thing I'll do is jump in the shower and wash off all these confusing emotions. Then I'll get the room ready and wait for her in the lobby. *Sounds like a plan.*

〜

"Yay! You're finally here!" I squeeze Sky until she almost pops. "Isn't this hotel amazing? Wait till you see the pool area and the beach."

"Careful—I stink. There was no AC in the fucking transfer bus." She steps back and ruffles her shirt. "I need to get these jeans off."

"Who cares." I grab her suitcase. "Let's go to our room so you can get settled. It's awesome!"

She glances around the lobby. "All I want to know is, where's the bar? I'm damn thirsty. It's been a fucking long day."

"Then let's get going. The faster you get your bathing suit on, the faster we can get to the bars before sunset." We walk to the elevator chatting like chickens, then I slap my forehead. "Oh, wait. We need to check you in first so you can get the bracelet you have to wear the entire week." I waggle the ugly florescent-yellow bracelet on my wrist.

Half an hour later we're in the lobby again, bothering the concierge with some questions and requests. Sky needs a million pillows to sleep on at night. Also, she forgot her eye mask to block out the sun. She may sound like she's high maintenance, but she's far from it.

The concierge gave us a brochure about day cruises we can take to other islands and told us to go to the marina that's owned by the hotel to make reservations. I scan the brochure while Sky asks the man about the spa. Each trip looks awesome. Finally, she's done.

"Okay. My pillows and mask are being delivered

as we speak," she announces. "Now let's go get a drink. This is taking forever."

"Before we go, look at these day cruises. Want to go on one?" We sift through the booklet and dog-ear two pages that look interesting. "We should go first thing in the morning to book one. The concierge says they book up fast."

"Sounds good to me. I really don't care what we do as long as we're in the sun. I checked my weather app, and it's already snowing at home. We're so lucky to be here!"

Just as we reach the doors, I drop my phone. It bounces off the marble floor. *Shit!* Sky picks it up and inspects it.

"You're damn lucky that didn't shatter on this hard floor," she says. "Put it away."

I examine it and tap the screen. No cracks or dents. "No worries. I've dropped this phone so many times. I'll put it away when we get to the pool."

We walk down the pathway lined with massive palm trees filled with coconuts, admiring the location. Suddenly, I tighten my grip around the phone and stop dead in my tracks. *Will. He's here?*

I can't contain my smile. My heart hammers in my chest. He has his sunglasses on again. I miss his eyes. He's changed his clothes to shorts and a yellow tank top, exposing a lot more skin. It's weird, though —I'm not getting the same vibe from him as I did on the plane. It's like he's a totally different person.

"Hey! Wh—what are you doing here?" I'd hug him, but my gut says not to.

At first I think he's going to walk right on by. Then he stops short next to us, looks around, then points his thumb at his chest. "I'm sorry, are you talking to me?"

What? I want to laugh, but it doesn't quite come out. "You're funny. I can't believe you're here. Your voice sounds so different." His eyebrows peek over his sunglasses. Goosebumps crawl up my arms and my smile fades.

"Well, I live and work here." He glances down at his phone.

I push my sunglasses up and prop them on my head to reveal my face. "Wow. You didn't tell me that. That's so cool." Of course he didn't. We really didn't share any personal things… which makes me cringe now.

He scratches his scruffy jaw. That's strange—he didn't have scruff on the plane. It couldn't have grown that fast. Come to think of it, his hair looks blonder too. But that's probably just because we're outside.

"I'm confused. Have we met? Have you been to this resort before?" He looks from me to Sky, then his head moves up and down. Is he checking her out? If I grip my phone any tighter, it's going to shatter.

"No, we haven't been here before," I respond with a nasty twang, hoping to regain his attention.

Sky squeezes my elbow. "Who is this guy?"

"Umm." Maybe I don't even know who he is.

His phone rings, and he takes a step back to answer it. "Hey. Yeah, I'm on my way. Bye." He ends the call, then glances at us as he walks backward. "Listen, I need to go."

I prop my hands on my hips. "Seriously? This is how you're going to act? Pretending like you don't know me? Real mature. I should've known better." Adrenaline rushes through my body, making me want to puke. How could I have kissed this guy's mouth?

"Lower your voice," Sky urges. "People can hear you. Let's go."

A group of women walk past, staring at us. He rubs his hand through his hair.

"This is nuts," he mutters and comes closer. "Listen, girlie. I have *never* seen you before in my life. You've obviously mistaken me for someone else. I'm sorry. I'm not him." Then he scurries away as if he can't wait to be out of sight.

Sky frowns at me. "What the hell was that all about? How could you possibly know someone here?"

"Give me a few minutes to cool down. I'll tell you at the pool." A lump is growing in my throat, and disappointment stabs me in the heart.

5

WILL

"Josh, where are you? I've just arrived at the marina." I hang my sunglasses from my shirt collar and walk behind the front counter to the office. It's a mess in here.

"Hey. Yeah, I'm on my way. Bye." That was short. Interesting.

A stack of papers and mail waits for me on the desk. Josh and I have been gone for ten days, and from the looks of our shared office, all hell broke loose. Apparently, most of the boats were rented, and the day cruises were all booked out.

That sounds good, but with both of us gone and another employee who got sick, things have been crazy. Not only did we have to cancel some cruises, but one motorboat broke down and almost sank. No one got hurt, but it wasn't easy for us on the back end. And dealing with all of this over the phone was a nightmare. Of course, it didn't help that my phone died today too.

I turn on my laptop and watch the screen light up. The password prompt appears, but I just stare at it. Work mode has not kicked in yet. My mind is only on Lacey. Not even Sawyer, which makes me feel like shit.

I couldn't walk away from her without knowing what it'd feel like to kiss her perfect lips. If circumstances were different, I would've asked her to dinner or to meet me for a drink. But I live in St. Thomas, and she's somewhere on vacation. She isn't someone I could be with for just a week. She'd be a forever kind of girl. But forever doesn't work with my lifestyle and career.

The bell rings as the front door opens. I lean back in my chair so I can see who it is. Josh walks around the counter toward the back.

"Hey, man." Josh and I fist bump. "Looks like you could use a beer or two, just like me."

He removes his sunglasses and lays them on his desk. "After being in frigid temps in New York, eighty-five degrees feels like a sauna. But I'd take this over that any day."

"Amen. I'm happy to be back too."

He cocks an eyebrow. "Did you finally get some sleep or something? You look much better than you did this morning, and you're not wearing your sunglasses inside. Back in the city, you were walking around like a gorilla with your arms dragging on the ground."

That's true. Sometimes I wonder why death affects everyone so differently. Two of the most important women in my life have been taken away from this earth too early and too suddenly. My mom, and now Sawyer's wife, Deb. She was like a sister to us. Sawyer, Deb, Josh, and I grew up together. I was closer to Sawyer and Deb than Josh was. It crushed Josh, but not as much as me. I think he mourns for a moment, gets it out of his system, and then he's good to go. *Wouldn't that be nice?*

"I asked Mike to stay a couple extra hours so I could take a shower and get some sleep."

He rolls his eyes. "How much did you have to pay him? Forty bucks?"

"I talked him down to thirty." He nods as if impressed, then rests his hands on the windowsill to look out at the boats.

"I wasn't sure I could sleep, but I don't remember hitting the pillow."

That's because of Lacey. Somehow, she helped relieve some of the pain in my heart and replaced it with a piece of her. How can I say that about someone I met on a plane and talked to for a couple of hours? She hardly even told me anything about herself. I know that she lives in the city, likes the Red Sox and Yankees, and her parents are divorced. I don't remember her last name, though.

Maybe it was the kiss. It sucked every sad emotion out of my body and filled me with pure lust, need, adoration… and something else I can't quite define. All I know is I walked out of the airport with a big smile on my face, not a scowl.

I check my phone to see if Lacey has sent me the picture of her yet. My heart sinks. Nothing. What do I expect? She's somewhere having fun. She's probably forgotten me already.

"Hey, is that your new one? Did you splurge and get the latest iPhone?"

"Yeah." I smile. "I said I wouldn't, but I gave in. It was time for an upgrade anyway." I unlock it and give it to him.

He fiddles around with it and checks out the camera. "Sweet. Because your phone died, I was bombarded with calls while I waited in the airport. Did ole man Jorge hook you up?"

"Yep. I went straight to his shop and, within minutes, the phone was in my hand, ready to go. I love it here."

"Me too, but man, there are some fucking weird guests at this resort right now." He gives me the phone back, then sits down. "Get this. Some chick with her friend stopped me on the way here, acting like she knew me. Then she got all pissed off when I told her I had no idea who she was. Almost as if we went on a date and I ignored her the next day."

"Well, that's you in a nutshell. So maybe you did go out with her." I'm joking, but I really kind of mean it.

"Not my type, but her friend was pretty hot." He motions with his hands that she had a big rack. "I would've liked to have known *her*."

"Not surprised. You love the lifestyle here because you know these women won't be around more than a week or two. There's never enough time for either one of you to get attached."

"Oh, and you never flirt with the guests here? Give me a break."

I shrug. "Not like you. We're thirty years old and you're still a dog. I should put a sign on the office door —'Beware of dog.' Don't you think it's time to start acting your age?"

He rubs his chin as he contemplates what I just said. "Nah. It's too much fun!" He laughs and I shake my head.

Josh has a new girlfriend every other day. Wait, I can't even call them girlfriends. Acquaintance is a better term. Me, on the other hand, I haven't met someone I like enough to go on a date. I've met some nice women here, but not anyone I wanted to pursue since they're always gone in a couple of days.

I'm the quieter, more serious one. Josh and I own this marina, Twin Anchors, along with our Uncle Leo, who also owns this resort. Josh and I run the show here, and making sure it's a success is more important to me than dating.

I have an MBA and a degree in advertising; Josh's degree is in marketing. I like the behind-the-scenes work, while he enjoys going out with the people— entertaining the guests and selling our services. It works for us.

He opens up his laptop and turns it on. "So how was your flight? No weirdos sitting next to you?"

I cough, then pick up the stapler and drop it in a desk drawer. Do I tell him about Lacey? I usually tell him everything. But I don't think I want to talk about that right now. He wouldn't take it seriously. And if I don't get the picture, there's no story to tell. I'll put her in the back of my mind and try to forget her. Maybe I'm making more out of it than what it was. I blame it on exhaustion.

Suddenly something smacks my forehead, then lands on my laptop keyboard. A Yankees stress ball. *What the hell?* I pick it up and whip it back at him like it's a real baseball.

He catches it and tosses it on his desk. "So what's up with you? You just zoned out."

"The flight was pretty bumpy. The people who sat around me were freaked out and green."

He laughs. "We're lucky we don't get motion sickness. We'd never be able to do what we do—we travel too much. Plus, water is our life."

"Yep. Thanks again for letting me take that early flight."

"You know me. I don't care. As long as I have my phone, music, or something to read, I'm good to go. As soon as you left, I went up to the executive lounge and waited patiently."

"Anyway, I need to wade through this stuff… clear off my desk. Can you do the rounds? There's a party of eight coming to pick up their motorboat early tomorrow."

"Which boat?"

"*White Pearl.* Slip twenty-five. It should be cleaned and stocked already." I hand him a clipboard. "Here's the paperwork for it."

He takes it and strolls to the door. "Oh!" He turns around. "Remember my senior prom date?"

Well, that's random. I scramble through my memory bank. "The one Chloe said looked like Reese Witherspoon, and we made her cry because we pretended I was you so you could run off with *my* date?"

Our sister was and still is obsessed with Reece Witherspoon—her movies and now her book club.

"Yes! I ran into her when we were in New York. I forgot to tell you the other day because of everything else that was going on."

"You didn't separate on good terms. Did she knee you in the nuts? Did you tell her you were me or you?"

He bursts out laughing. "Me. We aren't that much of assholes anymore. You aren't, anyway. But I did cover them just in case. She looked good—she's married with two kids."

I raise an eyebrow. "Why are you telling me this?"

"I don't know. The way that chick reacted to me today reminded me of all that shit we used to pull."

It took him another ten minutes to leave because we laughed about other ridiculous things we had done. Even to our parents and sister. But I guess that's what identical twins do.

6

LACEY

S ky had to drag me to the pool after Wi—*that guy* walked away. At first, I was stunned into silence, then mortification seeped in. I could've sworn he was Will. But now I'm questioning my own judgment. We were only together for a couple of hours. But we were face to face, lip to lip. We left the airport not too long ago. How could I have been so wrong?

"Hurry, look! Two people are leaving. Let's go before someone else snags those loungers!" Sky grabs my hand again and pulls me with her. We weave through narrow rows of white chairs. "And look, right by the swim-up pool bar. Bonus!"

We lay our towels on the chairs and take off our coverups. *Whoa!* "Awesome bikini, Sky. Love that mint-green color."

"Thanks. I'm on a green kick right now. It looks good with my olive skin and green eyes."

A lot of women are jealous of Sky. She has a gorgeous face to begin with and has one of the most beautiful bodies I've ever seen. Instead of running an art gallery, she should be a model. Her large breasts are naturally perky and her abs are perfect for the belly ring she wears. Guys describe her as tall and voluptuous. I tend to agree. She claims she's big boned. I've never been jealous of her before, but after I saw *that guy* checking her out, maybe I am now.

I take a deep breath and count to ten. Too many fucked-up emotions are screwing with my first day of vacation. I'll tell Sky everything to get it out of my system, and that'll be the last time I talk about Will.

The pool area is crowded and hopping. We sit on the edge of the pool and sway our legs through the water while we people watch. "Look at those guys playing water volleyball. Not a bad view from over here." Sky clicks her tongue. "You played volleyball in college. You should join in."

"I see your radar is on full blast already."

"Of course. Why shouldn't it be? I'm single, but I'm not looking to hook up here." She lifts a foot out of the water and wiggles her toes. "Check out my new toe ring. I saw a picture of Jennifer Aniston with one. It looked so sexy. What do you think?"

I nudge her with my elbow and chuckle. "Everything looks sexy on you. You have long, slender toes, so it looks good and it matches your style like your nose ring. Don't lose it in the pool, though. You'll never find it."

"Thanks," she says, then hops off the edge, splashing me. "Let's go."

We swim to the crowded bar and share a seat that

just became vacant. Do people leave because they see us coming, or is it pure luck? Our mouths drop open when we see the massive board with its long list of frozen drinks and their ingredients. My stomach growls. I'm not sure drinking is the best thing right now, but I don't care.

"I love that this resort is all-inclusive. We don't ever have to worry about money. Have I thanked you for finding this gem?"

"About a million times. We're only here for a week. That's not enough time to try all of these drinks, even if we share."

"Who the hell said I wanted to share?" I snicker.

She rests her sunglasses on the tip of her nose and her emerald eyes pierce mine. "After we order, you're going to explain to me what happened back there. Don't think I forgot about it. I'm too curious to let it go."

I huff. "Okay, okay." My shoulders slump in defeat. "Let's order something quickly before I chicken out. But let's go back to our chairs to talk about it. It's a long story."

"I *love* long stories." Sky waves down a bartender. "What are you in the mood for?"

Will.

"I don't know." I scan the board again. "Something with strawberries but no peaches or pineapples."

"Me too, but I'll make sure it's different than yours."

The bartender comes back in record time with our drinks. We toast to our first day.

"Holy shit." Sky's face contorts after she takes her first sip. "There's a lot of vodka in this. But it's so delicious," she says, slurping away.

I do the same. "We need to order some food. I'll be drunk before I finish this thing."

A couple other chairs have become free around us since it's late in the afternoon. We rearrange ours so we can face each other. The sun beats on our sides. That'll be funny if we get sunburned on opposite sides.

"Now that we've ordered some food, and we're relaxed and refreshed, I want every detail. Start from the beginning. Who did you think that hot guy was?"

"If you think he was good-looking, a guy that looked just like him sat in your empty seat on the plane."

"No way!" She taps my leg with her foot. "I got stuck sitting next to an old woman who smelled like mothballs and groaned all the time on the first flight. The second one was even more annoying. A teenage girl sat next to me and took a ton of selfies, then she started to whine to her mother because she didn't have Wi-Fi connection for Instagram and Snapchat. She's lucky I wasn't her mother."

I laugh. "Don't forget how we used to play with Snapchat a couple of years ago, and we're adults."

She nods, then waves her hand. "Enough of that. Story, please."

I take one more sip of my drink and begin. "Somehow I fell asleep before takeoff, and I didn't wake up until drinks were served. I don't remember him sitting down. When I woke up, I didn't pay much attention to him, but I felt this magnetic pull or tingling feeling. Like he was watching me—but not in a creepy way. I tried to check him out from the corner of my eye but couldn't see much. He wore sunglasses most of the time."

"Who wears sunglasses in an airplane? Anyway, did he say hello?"

"No. I just kept to myself, but that urge to talk to him was crazy. The silence started to feel awkward."

A waitress delivers a heaping plate of hummus and pita wedges to our table. We inhale it like we haven't eaten in days.

"So who broke it?" Sky asks, wiping hummus off the corner of her lip.

"Huh? Broke what?"

"The silence. Duh."

"Oh." I talk around a mouthful of food. "I did. You know me, I hate silence. I'd start a conversation with a tree."

She stirs her drink with a pink straw and smirks.

"Finally, I couldn't take it anymore. When I got a good look at him, my heart stopped. You can understand why."

"Ehh, he's hot but so not my type. Definitely yours, though. You know I like the artsy ones with ink."

"I'm glad you know my type because sometimes I don't even know what that is. It's been so long since I've been with anyone I was excited about. This is a whole new level of attraction for me."

I look at Sky and burst out laughing.

She sits up and looks around. "What happened? What's so funny?"

"Are you going to eat that?"

"Eat what?" She inspects the hummus. "Is there something in it?"

I point to her chest and chuckle again. "Don't you feel the piece of strawberry that's sitting so nicely in your cleavage?"

She looks down and scoops it out like it's a bug. "Damn boobs. This is something that usually happens to you, not me."

"What? I don't have big boobs for things to fall on and get comfortable there!"

She cleans off her chest with a napkin. "You know what I mean."

"Yeah, I do, because my story gets better. He got a sample of the stupid shit that happens to me—I spilled a bloody mary on my sweatshirt." I proceed to tell her about that and getting my backpack stuck on a seat and then banging into the bathroom door.

She covers her mouth to prevent herself from laughing.

"It was so embarrassing. I know he was watching me, because that zing followed me all the way to the bathroom."

"He was checking out your ass." She wiggles her eyebrows.

"He didn't see much because my sweatshirt covered everything. Anyway, you should've seen me in the cramped bathroom while the plane was bouncing around and attendants were banging on the door, demanding I go back to my seat. Mints were rolling all over the floor."

"Mints? What the hell were you doing eating mints in the bathroom?"

"I didn't want to go back to him with tomato-juice breath. Gross. What's even worse, I lost my balance and fell onto the toilet when I tried to get my legs through my shorts." I scan my legs and arms for bruises.

"Eww! That's just disgusting."

"The lid was down, so it wasn't so bad. Once I was finished, I doused myself with antibacterial hand gel. I smelled like a hospital when I got back to my seat." I shake my head and laugh. "Man, my life is like a TV show. I wish it were taped. You'd all be laughing at my expense."

She takes off her sunglasses and wipes her finger under her eyes. "Your stories always make me laugh until I cry. Okay, enough of the bathroom. I want to go take a shower with scalding hot water. What happened next?"

"Turbulence played a hand *again*—this time in my favor. When I returned to my seat, I lost my balance and fell on top of him." I twist in my chair to show her the position I was in.

"No, you didn't!" She buries her face in her hands. "You're such a fucking mess."

I turn back around. "He didn't seem to mind because he wrapped his arms around my waist instead of tossing me on my seat like a hot potato."

She perks up in her chair. "Ooh. Did he have big hands? I love big hands."

"Just listen." My anger against the Will lookalike is decreasing while I replay everything. It's changing into the warmth I felt when I was next to Will on the plane.

"So then, I said I was cold, and he took off his sweatshirt and gave it to me. Then he took my hands in his big mitts to warm them."

"So they *were* big."

"He played baseball in college. Do your hands have to be big for that? If so, yes, his hands were big."

"Love it. You didn't mind him touching you, though? It would've irked me."

"That's what I'm trying to say. It was so natural. I've never been more comfortable with a guy."

She nods slowly. "Who you didn't know."

I nod and eat the last pita square. "Right. What's your point?"

"He had his sunglasses on the whole time? He sounds shady to me."

"I asked him to take them off."

She takes her own sunglasses off and leans forward. "And?"

"Better than I expected."

I describe his eyes to her, then how we took a selfie.

"Wait! I can show you. Then you'll see how much he looks like that other guy."

I take my phone out and sift through my pictures. I took a bunch at the resort while I was waiting for

Sky to arrive. My heart warms when I see the pictures of us. He's so damn cute.

"This is him."

She reaches out for my phone, then sits back again. "Holy shit. It's scary how much they look alike. They say there's a doppelganger out there for everyone. But this other guy might look completely different without the sunglasses."

"True. But to see them on the same day? I wish I had a picture of him with his sunglasses on."

"Wait a second. Why didn't you tell me this when I first arrived?"

I put my empty cup next to hers on the table and shrug. "I wasn't sure if I was going to tell anybody. I wanted it to be my little secret."

"What for? It's not like you joined the mile-high club."

"I know. I wanted to avoid anything love related while I'm here, and then he got your empty seat. It couldn't have been a bigger surprise."

"Back up a second. You didn't talk about where you lived or what you did for a living? Nothing personal like that?"

"No. It's hard to explain. It's as if we already knew all that stuff about each other. I wanted to kiss him like I did it all the time."

"So how did you leave it?"

I tell her how we almost kissed toward the end of the flight. The awkwardness that followed.

Screaming and whistling from the pool grabs my attention. "It looks like volleyball's getting out of hand with all that muscle, testosterone, and alcohol. Why aren't there any women playing?"

"Who cares. Back to the story. So you separated and nothing else?" She presses her lips together and looks disappointed. "That kind of pisses me off. I would've expected more by the way you're acting."

"Chill. I'm not finished yet." I tap my fingertips together and flash an evil smile.

She sits up in her chair again. "Spill it. Now."

"I thought I lost him after customs. Then, get this!" I pause, remembering.

Her eyes widen. "What?"

"He yanked me into a corner and kissed me. Soft at first, but within seconds, *bam*, we devoured each other, knowing that it was our one and only kiss."

"And?" Her hand waves me on to continue.

I deflate in my chair. "He disappeared."

She throws her napkin on the empty hummus dish. "Well, now I'm even more pissed off. You just let a hot lip-devourer get away like that? You didn't give him your number? Oh, but *you* have *his* number. The ball's in your court. Are you going to send him the picture?"

I sigh and fiddle with my nails. "I don't know. I've been fighting with myself since I left the airport. What if I send it and he doesn't respond? What if I do send it and he responds, but he turns out to be a deadbeat? I want to look back at this experience and say, 'wow,' not 'shit, what the hell was I thinking?'"

"I can't believe you. This isn't high school anymore. How many times have I seen you tell someone to take a risk for their relationship? To jump in headfirst and see where it takes them? But what are you doing? The complete opposite! There's nothing wrong with lust on vacation. Live a little."

"Maybe that's not what I'm looking for with him. It was more than that. Let me think about it until tomorrow. I have to follow my gut and right now, it's saying don't send it."

"Hey, lovely ladies." We turn our heads toward a deep flirty voice. Two wet pretty-boys are propped on the edge of the pool. One's holding a ball in his hand and shining his pearly whites at us. The other guy looks over the edge of his sunglasses at Sky. "Want to play water volleyball?"

"Come on." I slap her knee playfully. "Let's go kick their asses."

"But my boobs are going to fly out of my top," she mumbles.

"Even better. They'll be staring at them while the ball flies right past them. Easy win."

7

WILL

The sound of waves slapping against the dock is one of my favorite things. I've missed it since we were gone. Every morning I come to the office earlier than the others and have my coffee outside to enjoy the peace and quiet before the long days begin. This morning, I only had ten minutes alone.

It wasn't my goal to end up in St. Thomas, but through all the twists and turns of life, it has become a blessing. I'd be happy with this forever.

Ever since Josh and I were little, the water has been our second home. We vacationed at the Hamptons every summer and went there as much as possible during the other months. My parents loved sailing, and that love turned into a passion for us. Not for our sister, Chloe, though. She prefers city life. My dad's best friend, Joe, owns a marina in the Hamptons, and Josh and I worked there every summer during high school and college. That's how we learned the ins and outs of running one.

After we'd gotten our degrees, Joe asked us if we'd be interested in buying the marina or becoming partners. Running the marina was becoming too much for him since he was getting older. He wanted the business to stay in the family, but his son didn't want to take it over. We were the next best option. After a lot of tough discussions and planning, we said yes. Then a couple years later, Uncle Leo approached us about St. Thomas.

Long story short, we now live half the year in St. Thomas and the other half in the Hamptons. We get the best of both worlds—Joe runs the marina in the Hamptons during the winter, and we take over during the summer high season. That also gives us a chance to visit with family while we're in the north. It hasn't been easy, but we've made it work.

My shirt is already soaked from sweat. It's going to be a bitch today. I'm exhausted because I was on the phone with Sawyer until late. All he keeps saying is how love sucks and I should never fall in love. I can understand why he says this because I saw the torment Dad went through when Mom died.

I feel like shit that I'm down here. His parents don't live in the city, and he has no siblings. Josh and I are the closest to brothers he has. I wish I could be there for him, but life goes on and I have to work. I'll be closer to him in July, when Josh and I move back to the Hamptons.

The first group of the day shows up for the motorboat they've rented. I get the paperwork all signed, walk them out to the boat and give them some instructions, then send them off on their adventure. It's a newlywed couple extending their honeymoon with some friends. They stayed at the hotel alone for a few days before their friends came down. They're headed out to the British Virgin Islands for a week now. One of my favorite places in the world.

Buzz. "Will," Josh calls over the walkie-talkie.

Buzz. "I'm here. What's up?"

Buzz. "Can you watch the front desk for a few minutes? Mike's busy with one of the boats, and Molly doesn't come in for another hour. I need to check on something for the tour that starts in thirty minutes. Oh, and that chick I told you about from yesterday is roaming the marina with her friend. I'm not in the mood."

Buzz. "So that's the real reason you want to escape." I laugh.

Buzz. "Yeah. It's too early, and I haven't had my coffee yet."

Buzz. "Why would it make a difference if she sees me instead of you? I'm your twin. She'll still think I'm you."

Buzz. "So pretend you're not."

Buzz. "What?" My voice squeaks. "That doesn't even make sense. I'm getting too old for this shit. I don't know why you even care."

Buzz. "Just cover for me if they come to the desk."

Buzz. "Fine. I want you back in ten minutes. I have a lot to do today and standing behind the counter isn't one of them."

Buzz. "I owe you. Thanks!"

I don't respond and hook my walkie-talkie to my shorts. With my checklist in hand, I head back to the office. I stop along the way to fix a rope connected to a dinghy. I hear some giggles.

"Look at the size of this vessel! It's huge," one woman says.

I freeze and stay low. *Wait a second. Is that—* I eavesdrop some more. My stomach clenches with excitement.

"What kind of vessel are we talking about here? A boat or something else?" They both burst out laughing.

"You're sick." More laughter.

"Yeah, but that's why I'm so much fun."

I'd know that perky voice anywhere. I stand up and walk around one of the large boats. My breath hitches. Blond hair with pink streaks mingles with the sea breeze, revealing her slender bare back. Her giggles find their way over to me. I can't believe she's here.

Buzz. "I'm on my way back. Is the coast clear?" *Shit!* This damn thing is so loud.

Both girls turn around at the same time. Lacey pushes her hair away from her face with her sunglasses.

"Lacey? I can't believe you're here." My first instinct is to hug her, but I don't follow through when her face morphs into anger.

She props her hands on her hips. "Are you mental? Yesterday, you said you'd never seen me before when I ran into you on the way to the pool.

And suddenly you remember my name? Maybe you are a drug addict with your shady sunglasses."

Fuck. She's the girl Josh was talking about.

"Lacey, it was all a misunderstanding. I can exp—"

"There you are. Why didn't—? Oh." Josh has arrived.

I remove my cap and sunglasses, and so does Josh. Lacey's mouth drops wide open. Her eyes dart from me to him. Her friend's head bobs all over the place, not knowing where to look.

"There's t—two of you?" She points her finger at us and takes one step back and then another.

I stretch out my arms and hop forward. "Watch out!"

She squeals and flails her arms. We all scream at the same time and watch Lacey fall backward into the water. *Fuck!* I drop my stuff on the ground, yank the walkie-talkie off my shorts, and swiftly take off my shoes. Then I dive in after her.

Her arms flap everywhere as she gasps for air, splashing water into my face. I pull her into my arms. Her legs wrap around my waist. I'm glad I'm wearing cargo shorts instead of thin swim trunks. For a split second I think of her in my arms in the plane.

"Breathe." Her sunglasses hang off her chin. She pushes the hair away from her face and wipes the water from her eyes. She moves her head back when she realizes how close our faces are. Her gaze caresses my lips. "I've got you. You're lucky there wasn't a boat in the slip."

Her eyes spit fire, and she pushes me away. "I used to be a lifeguard. I can swim, thank you very much." She shoves her sunglasses into her wet hair on the top of her head.

"I was just trying to help you."

"I don't need your help," she snaps.

"Lace… Lace… one of your flip-flops is floating right behind you. Grab it before it sinks," her friend shouts and points. Lacey twists around and smacks the water when she grabs it.

"Throw it to me," her friend instructs. She whips it at her.

"Great arm. Did you ever play softball?"

She glares at me. Okay, not the time to make jokes. She looks back at her friend.

"It doesn't matter if you have one of them, because I don't see the other one anywhere. I can't walk around with one damn flip-flop!"

Her friend walks along the border of the slip, searching for the other one. "Sorry, I don't see it either."

A pink flip-flop floats nearby. "Here it is!" I hold it up in the air.

"Throw it up here," Josh says. I toss it to him like a frisbee.

"How do I get out of the water?" Lacey grouses. "Is there a ladder somewhere?" She spins around in search of one.

"Yes. Follow me."

We swim over to it, then I stop. "Ladies first."

She mimics me while she climbs up with no problem. Of course, I had a nice show of her ass on the way up. I won't complain. Her friend meets us by the ladder and hands us towels that Josh fetched for us. She drops Lacey's flip-flops on the ground for her to put on. Lacey dries her face, then wrings out her long hair.

I walk away to give them some space. Josh picks up my stuff and brings it over to me. My wet shorts feel like they weigh a hundred pounds, and my shirt clings to me like plastic wrap. I peel it off and drop it on the ground with a splat. I quickly dry off and toss the towel onto my shirt. I always have spare clothes in the office.

"That was one hell of an introduction. I can't believe you know her." Josh mumbles. "It should've registered that she might have been talking about you. It didn't dawn on me because we just got back yesterday."

"I sat next to her on the plane. I'll tell you about it later. Damn, she's pissed off."

"Did you know she was staying at this resort?"

"No! Now shut up."

They come toward us, but they're busy talking. Lacey looks at me, and suddenly her body language completely changes. Her eyes flash and drift slowly down my chest to my abs and back up again. She rubs her neck, then drops her hand to her chest. I like what I see, and so does she. Her wet hair falls over one shoulder. Her black bikini top clings to her breasts, scrambling my mind. Her cut-off jeans cling to her slick, toned legs. I've never seen a sexier woman. And I've seen my fair share.

"Th—thanks for the towel," she says nervously. I take it from her and drop it on mine.

"Lacey, this is my twin brother, Josh. He's the one you ran into yesterday."

Her friend smiles and gives a slight wave. "Just in case you're wondering, I'm Skylar. But people call me Sky. As I told Lacey yesterday, there's a twin out there for everyone, but who knew?" She shakes our hands.

"This is amazing," Lacey says. She's looking me and Josh up and down. "At a quick glance, there's no telling you two apart. I thought your voice sounded different yesterday, but…" She puts a hand on her hip and steps sideways, toward me. "There are two things I noticed about you on the plane. Let me see if you're really who you claim to be. If you are Will, you have a tiny birthmark behind your left ear and gold specks in your right eye."

I bend my neck to the right and try not to smile. She stands on tiptoe and traces the birthmark lightly, then trails her soft finger down my neck. I wonder what her lips would feel like instead of her fingers.

She goes over to Josh but doesn't touch him. She knows he's not me. This is all a game.

"Nothing on you. Now the eyes." She checks Josh first. "Nope."

"See. I said I didn't know you," he remarks. Skylar shakes her head.

"Josh!" I warn.

"What?" He backs away with his hands up.

Lacey stands in front of me again. I gaze into her eyes. Their color is even more stunning in the sun. Just like I imagined.

"Your eyes look beautiful in the sunlight. I could never forget you."

Her mouth quirks at the corners and then my phone rings. I growl. Timing fucking sucks. This better be important. I pat down my shorts, in search of my new phone that is thankfully waterproof. I pull it out and shake the water off it. Sawyer's name flashes across the screen. My shoulders droop and my mood changes. I shift my eyes to Josh. "It's Sawyer. I have to take this.

"Excuse me for a second," I say to Lacey.

"Hey, Sawyer." He mumbles *Deb* and something else. I hope he isn't drunk this early in the morning. "Give me a second.

"Lacey, Skylar, I'm sorry. I have to take this call. Can you stay around for a little while? This shouldn't take too long." I only focus on Lacey to see her reaction.

"No... we can't. We have plans," Lacey says robotically. Skylar's forehead wrinkles. Her mouth opens like she wants to say something, but she doesn't.

I grab Lacey's hand and the now-familiar surge of heat pulses through my veins, practically drying my shorts in an instant. "Will you come back? When can I see you again?"

"Will, Sawyer's waiting," Josh interrupts.

I'd make Josh talk to Sawyer, but he's not good at

giving a sympathetic shoulder. He'd just hand the phone back to me.

Lacey gently tugs her hand away. "I don't know." She motions to Skylar. "Come on, Sky. Let's go."

"We're here all week," Skylar blurts out. Lacey's elbow jabs her side.

Buzz. Both our walkie-talkies go off. I clench my jaw.

"Will or Josh, can one of you come give me a hand at slip twelve?" Mike says on the other end. *Welcome back to work.*

Josh pats me on the shoulder, then answers Mike and walks off.

I glance at Lacey one more time before she disappears. If she won't come back, I'm going to have to track her down somehow.

"Why are we leaving? It was obviously a stupid misunderstanding," Sky says once we're out of sight. "And we didn't even book a cruise."

"Do you know how embarrassing it was to fall in the water? Why does this shit always happen to me? And then finding out it was his twin brother yesterday. Then I stared at Will's bare chest like he's a Greek god. He's hot as hell, dry and soaking wet. Oh, and I don't even want to mention his happy trail. It's all too tempting and too much."

"Would you stop for a minute and look at me?" Sky blocks me like a football player.

I look over my shoulder to make sure we're far enough from the marina. "What do you want from me? I need to go back to the hotel and change my shorts."

"I can understand why you're upset, but didn't you see the way he lit up when he first saw you? If the sun fell into the ocean, the smile on his face would light up the entire planet instead. His jaw clenched so tightly when you traced your finger down his neck. It wasn't from anger. Even I could see your chemistry is off the charts."

We continue to walk again and follow the path to the beach. Screw my shorts. They'll dry in the sun. I forgot my sunscreen, though. Not good.

"I told you——we can't seem to keep our hands off each other. When he grabbed me in the water, I wrapped my legs around his waist without even thinking about it. It's like we're two magnets or something. I guess it scares me a little bit. I hardly know anything about him."

We kick off our flip-flops and step on the soft sand. Walking with any type of shoes on sand is a pain in the ass. I follow her toward the water.

She turns around to face me and walks backward. "So what? Have some fun. I'm jealous. I wish I was that attracted to someone. My heart's been broken way too many times. Men only want one thing from me, and that's sex. I've had my fun too, but I need a break from the dating scene. If a guy seems interested here, then maybe I'll hang out with him, but I'm not going out of my way. Always hopeful, but always let down."

"Well, that's all this might be too. This is new territory for me. I'm usually the one watching others get together or fall in lust. Now it's happening to me, and I don't have a clue what to do."

She turns around and says, "You're making it more complicated than it is."

We plop down on the sand, not too far from the water. Knowing me, I'll get plowed over by a huge wave. I bury my feet in the damp sand and toss my flip-flops behind me so they don't get sucked up by the water. Sky's land next to mine.

"Do you still want to go water-skiing with the guys from last night? We're supposed to meet them in an hour. We don't have to go. I couldn't care less either way."

"Of course I want to go, with or without them. Water-skiing is a blast. My pride won't ruin our vacation. I promise… and that's all I'm going to say."

"Good." She rubs sand off her hands.

I drop my head back and let the ocean breeze dry my hair. It's a tangled mess at this point. How can some people hate the beach? I can relax and breathe here. The city is overpopulated, hectic, and the air quality is horrible. I could wear a bathing suit all year round. My job would be irrelevant here, though. I'm not sure Jocelyn would let me telecommute. Why am I even thinking about this? Probably because I'm on vacation. Maybe I'd get sick of it after a while.

"So, I have some news," Sky says, her eyes dancing. "I'm trying not to get too excited about it, in case it falls through."

"What's up?" *My skin's burning.*

"The art gallery I work for in Boston wants to open a small one in New York City. My boss asked if I'd be interested in relocating to manage it." She squeals. Then I squeal and get a chunk of still-wet hair in my mouth. *Yuck!* I sit up and pull it all into a braid to control it.

"Holy shit! That means you would live in the city. We could hang out all the time. I'm so excited." I wrap my arm around her shoulder and squeeze her tight. "Congratulations."

"Thanks. I'm thrilled, but nothing's in writing yet. My boss asked me to go to the city when we get back to look at some spaces that are for rent. The new gallery will focus only on photography, which you know I love. She's still throwing around ideas."

"Why didn't you tell me sooner?"

She shrugs. "We've been occupied with Will since we got here. I had a feeling you might want to talk about something else now. Perfect opportunity."

I cringe. "Man, do I suck. I'm sorry. No more talking about Will." She raises an eyebrow because she knows I'm full of shit. "When would you need to move? Three or four months?" I lean back on my hands.

"No, earlier than that. Which is crazy because I don't have a place to live. It's so damn expensive in New York."

"My apartment is small, but you can crash with me until you find something. You'd have to sleep on the couch, though. But without all the pillows! It'd be fun to have a roommate again."

"Seriously?" She slaps her hands together, and somehow, I get covered in sand. I sit up, spitting and wiping off my face. My lips are rough like I'm giving them a sugar scrub.

"I'm so sorry!" she exclaims.

I stand up and wipe off my shorts. "No worries. Now my lips are soft and kissable. Let's go wade in the water. My skin is going to fry off." She follows me.

"What was I saying?" The waves splashing against my legs are so refreshing. "Oh, yeah. Yes. I'm serious about you staying with me, but you'll have to clean up after yourself. You know I'm a little bit of a neat freak. Look at our hotel room. Your shit is everywhere, and we've been here less than twenty-four hours." I poke fun at her.

"I promise I'll *try* to be neater and more orga- nized. I don't want to intrude on your privacy, but you're the only one I know there."

"What privacy? Like I have guys coming and going all the time. Now I'll have someone to watch Netflix with or share a gallon of ice cream or a bottle of wine, instead of me drinking it by myself." I flick water at her with my foot. "And I'm not the only one you know. How about Drew and Christian? They're your brothers too. You've met Christian's wife, Joce- lyn, a couple of times too. She's sweet as can be, and she'll suck you into the family whether you like it or not."

"No, they're *your* brothers. I've never gotten that warm feeling from them like I do from you."

"Whatever. Don't worry about them. You might not be blood related to us, but we're tied by marriage. You're part of our family, and we aren't easy to get rid of."

"Don't make me cry. I've always wanted sisters

and brothers. You feel more like a friend, so you'll need to remind me that you're my stepsister. I hate saying that. It makes me think of Cinderella and her wicked stepsisters. You're far from it."

"Does it scare you to move? You've lived in the Boston area your entire life."

"I'm twenty-eight, and I'm bored with Boston. It's time to experience something exciting, make new friends, change my surroundings."

"I'd love to have a chance to do that, but I don't know if I'd have the guts."

I'm twenty-seven and wish for the same thing. Is this the age when people start to question their lives and look at what they've accomplished? My parents always said they got married too young and didn't really know what they wanted to do. Then divorce happened because, when they figured it out, they wanted different things. But if they didn't get divorced and remarried, I wouldn't be sitting here with Sky right now. And I wouldn't have met Will.

I splash water over my shoulders, then pat down my arms with my wet hands. *Sunburn alert*. "Let's celebrate your pending promotion tonight. We should dress up and go to the dance club in the resort. I'm not usually much of a dance club person, but let's try it out anyway."

"Sounds good to me. Hey, I need to go back to the room before we go water-skiing."

I follow her out of the water and pick up my flip-flops. "Me too. I want to put my hair up, and I forgot to put on sunscreen. I'll be red as a lobster tonight if I don't do it."

"Tomorrow we're going back to the marina to book one of those day cruises. Even if Will or his brother are there. Understand?"

"Yes, Mom."

"Will! Josh! Whoever you are! Stop for a second."

I turn around, and I'm surprised to see Skylar walking toward me, waving her hand. Lacey's not with her. I slip my clipboard under my arm and run my hand through my hair.

"Hi, Skylar. You've found Will." I smile at her.

"Good. You're who I wanted to talk to. Please, call me Sky."

"Sure. Want to sit down for a minute?" I motion to the bench next to the office building. "How was your day? I couldn't tell if Lacey was upset or not. Hmm… maybe she is, since she's not with you."

"She doesn't know I'm here. I snuck out of our room when she fell asleep."

My thoughts go back to watching her sleep on the plane. She's probably even more adorable now.

"Water-skiing and being in the sun knocked us out. I think she would've skied all day if she could've."

She winces. "Her back and shoulders got pretty burned."

"Do you want to book a cruise or something?"

"Yes, and I came for another reason." Her eyes glimmer with mischief.

"Okay. Shoot."

"Lacey told me all about you. Actually gushed about you, but don't tell her I told you that. She'd kill me. She was mortified today and yesterday, as it is. You can understand why."

I nod.

"But the funny thing is, if it weren't you today, she wouldn't have given a shit. She would've laughed her ass off because things like that happen to her all the time."

"Why does she care so much now?"

"Because she likes you, dummy. It's not that she wants to impress you. I think everything was a bit much. Falling in the water, finding out you have an identical twin, and that you work here. You know what I mean?"

"Yes, but seeing her again caught me off guard too. In a good way, though. She shouldn't be upset about a misunderstanding that I had no control over."

"How do you feel about her? Do you want to see her again?" She lifts her hand. "You know what? Don't answer that. We're going to Copper Cove tonight with a couple of guys we met."

I press my lips together. *Thanks for stabbing me in the heart and twisting it.* Why am I jealous? I have no claim over her.

"One guy seems interested in her, but her heart and mind are somewhere else. I think you know where. Why don't you stop by and see for yourself? Bring Josh if you want. I can help him find a date for the night," she offers with a cheeky grin.

I said I was going to go after her. This is the opening I needed.

"I'll think about it. Thanks for letting me know. Come with me to the front desk so I can look at the calendar."

"Sounds good."

"Tell me why we're here. You never want to go to dance clubs, especially to this place," Josh nags.

I ignore him and survey the room. If Lacey's not here, there's no reason to stay. I'll suggest we have a drink and leave. It's like a maze in here, trying to get to the bar. The music isn't too loud yet. The dance floor on the other side of the club is only half full. I weave in between people and say polite hellos to the hotel personnel I know. Josh is no longer behind me because he's chatting with a couple of women who were at the marina today.

He wouldn't get off my ass about Lacey, so I had to tell him the quick version of our story. I didn't tell him about Skylar's visit. He isn't the easiest person to talk to about relationship stuff. If that's what this is. He did listen without interrupting, which was surprising. He told me if I feel something for her, then I should go after her. Not many people get a second chance. Then he changed the subject.

He brought up how I always drop what I'm doing to help other people. When Sawyer called and told me about Deb, I was on a plane that day. When Mom died, I gave up baseball after college to be home with my family and pick up the broken pieces. Josh and Chloe did too, but I always initiate everything and they follow.

I'm not someone to back down from getting what I want, unless I have to. After I saw Lacey again today and noticed how much my body and heart responded to hers, I know she's who I want. Which is crazy because I hardly know her.

I'm almost to the bar when I see her. I freeze. She's chatting with Skylar and some guys. Her arms are moving like they did when she fell into the water. They all start to laugh. Maybe she's telling them the story.

I stand where I have a perfect view of her. A loose braid pulls her hair away from her exposed shoulders in her strapless top. Thin tendrils of blond and pink relax against the sensuous curve of her neck. I don't know if it's the lighting in here, but her skin is pretty red. Skylar mentioned something about sunburn.

Mac, the bartender, approaches me. We shake hands. "Hi, Will. Haven't seen you around the hotel for a while. Glad you're here."

"Thanks. I had to fly up north for a couple of weeks. There was a death in the family."

"Dude. I'm sorry."

I shrug. "Thanks. It's life, right?"

He nods with sympathy. "What can I get you?"

"Any Frenchtown beer you have on tap."

"You got it."

With my hip against the side of the bar, I rest my elbow on top. Lacey's face is lit up as she chats away like she did on the plane. But then she stops to take a sip of her martini and glances in my direction. Her eyes spring open, and she almost drops her glass on the bar; red martini splashes on her hand. She knows it's me, not Josh. She licks her finger innocently, and every nerve in my body lights up.

The guy next to her follows her gaze and scowls at me, then whispers something in her ear. She doesn't respond and leans away from him. Skylar looks over her shoulder and acknowledges me by lifting her chin.

"Here's your beer. Try to stick around awhile. Jimmy'll be right back. He'd love to see you."

"Thanks." I place some money on the bar. I don't have to pay for drinks here, but I always leave a tip.

I remain in my spot for a while. We glance at each other several times. A smile here, a giggle there. I guess she's not mad or embarrassed anymore.

Josh claps me on the back. "I should've known why you wanted to come here. I wouldn't mind hanging out with Skylar, if you and Lacey want to run off somewhere."

"I have a feeling Skylar won't fall for your bullshit, so watch out."

"You know me. I'm always up for a challenge. Did you talk to Lacey?"

"No. I'm fine where I am. She knows I'm here."

"The guy next to her seems pretty determined. Arm around the back of her chair." He stretches his neck. "He just put his hand on her knee, and she brushed it off."

Jealousy kicks in again. "I guess he hasn't noticed her looking over here the entire time rather than at him."

She hops off her chair and hooks arms with Skylar. They say something to the guys and walk away. Lacey looks over her shoulder and gives me a sexy smirk. She angles her head faintly and motions for us to follow. I chug the rest of my beer, and we catch up to them just as they reach the bathroom doors. They press against the adjacent wall, hiding themselves.

"What are you doing?"

"Those guys were cramping our style, so we said we had to go to the bathroom. Girls always travel in pairs," Skylar explains. Like men don't know that by now.

"Want to help us escape?" Lacey begs.

I reach out my hand for her to take it. "Come with me." She extends her arm, then hesitates. "I don't bite."

"But maybe I do. We're not on the plane anymore. This is a whole new ballgame." *Feisty.* One more thing that makes her even more attractive.

"Let's see who wins." I waggle my eyebrows, then snag her hand. "Let's go."

We bolt out the door and follow a path lined with

sparkling solar lights. Skylar and Josh are chatting away behind us, but I can't make out what they're saying.

"Hey, guys," Skylar says. "Josh and I are going to the bar by the lobby. Don't worry. I'll make sure he behaves." She punches him in the arm playfully. He rubs the spot with his hand, then pretends he's going to hit her back.

Lacey gives Josh the evil eye.

"I'm just kidding," he says. "I'll behave. I'll try to anyway."

Skylar gives Lacey a hug. They don't say anything, but they don't have to. We all know they're doing it so we can be alone. We wave to them as they walk away.

I take both her hands in mine. "Lacey, are you okay with this? Are we okay? We didn't part on the best of terms this morning."

She rocks on her heels and flashes me the smile I love. "More than okay. I was hoping they'd leave us alone." *Me too*.

"What would you like to do? Walk on the beach? There's a small bar with couches and tables at the end of this path."

"I want you alone, but somewhere that there's a little bit of light. I want to see you, not the darkness, when we talk. Too bad we missed the sunset."

"I have an idea. Come with me." We walk to the end of the path. "Stay here for a second. Would you like a drink?"

"Just water, please."

I kiss her cheek before I head to the bar. The

bartender shakes my hand when he sees me. I ask him for a couple of things. He nods and walks away.

Lacey looks out at the ocean with her hands clasped in front of her. Wisps of her hair blow gently in the breeze. Her black capris hug her backside, exposing her sexy curves. The shade of pink from her shirt blends with the rosiness of her skin. This beautiful woman wants to be alone with me tonight. How did I get so lucky for the second time?

The bartender comes back with a bag and hands it to me.

"Thanks, man. You're the best. I'll bring this stuff back later."

"No problem. I know where you live." He laughs and turns away to help a customer.

I walk back to Lacey. "Okay. I've got what we need."

"What are you up to?" She tries to peek in the bag, but I hold it behind my back.

"You have to wait and see. Let's go out on the beach where the sun loungers are."

She laces her fingers with mine. "Lead the way."

We walk along the boardwalk that leads to the hotel's private beach. Loungers line up in pairs, each with a wooden table and a straw sun umbrella between them. We remove our shoes before we step onto the sand.

"There's nothing better than the feeling of sand on your feet or between your toes." She sighs. "You get to do this every day. I'm envious."

"Definitely one of the perks of living here." I stop next to two chairs. "How about here?"

"Sure, but it's dark. I'd rather see your handsome face since you're not hiding behind your sunglasses now."

"Luckily I thought ahead. Give me a few seconds to set up."

I remove two water bottles and three table lanterns from the bag. I place the lanterns strategically on the table. The breeze is calm so they're easy to light.

"Can you see me now?"

"This is perfect, and the chairs even have cushions. I hope my sunburn doesn't show as much. My skin hasn't been exposed to this kind of sun in a long time."

"Does it hurt?"

"A little bit. It's mostly on my back. But who cares."

We sit down sideways on the chairs, facing each other instead of lying back. She rubs her hands between her legs and then looks up to the sky.

"The stars are amazing here. So far, everything has been. Much better than I could've imagined."

I rub her knee to get her attention. "Even after this morning?"

"After my ego cooled off, I couldn't get my mind around the fact that you were at this hotel too. I'm surprised you were at the dance club. That doesn't seem like your scene."

"It's not, and it wasn't a coincidence. A little birdy

told me you'd be there. Since you walked away from me this morning, I knew I had to go after you. She gave me the perfect opening."

She shakes her head. "Sky! She's such a sneak. But I love her for it."

"I heard you're an awesome water-skier."

She laughs. "Not awesome, but I ski okay. I only wiped out once. It's been years since I've done it, but it came right back, just like riding a bike. I love anything water or beach related. I think I was a beach bum in a prior life."

She stands up from her chair and wipes off her pants. "Scoot over. I don't like being so far away from you."

"Wait a second. Don't sit down yet."

I fix the back of the lounger so I can sit upright. I'm glad there are no arms on these things. I sit down with my legs split and hanging over the edges. Without saying anything, she sits facing me, with her legs resting on top of mine. She's not on my lap but close enough.

"Is this okay?" she says softly. Her eyes glisten from the lanterns.

"No matter how close you are to me, it will never be close enough," I murmur. A smile blooms on her face.

My hands grip her hips, and I pull her closer. Her tiny hands rest on my upper arms. I don't know how long I'll be able to withstand kissing her again.

"My body feels this strange tingling sensation when you're nearby. It's like there's a lasso wrapped around my heart, and your heart holds the rope. And I don't know what to think or do about it," she murmurs.

My need for her spikes, and I sit up straight, tugging her onto my lap. My heart hammers as I skim my thumbs along the sweep of her cheeks. She leans closer and nods like she's reading my mind.

All restraint disappears, and my lips mesh with hers. Our mouths open and tongues join as we surrender to our desires. Her hands brush through my hair as my fingers trace down her lower back. We kiss with heated passion like we've been apart for a lifetime. She rubs her breasts against my chest, and I ache to touch every part of her body. We both moan in delight as she rocks against me. Before things get too out of hand, I steady her and pull away.

Her eyelids flutter open. Our chests rise and fall in the same rhythm.

"It kills me to stop because I want you more than anything." My mouth captures hers again. "But if we're going to take this any further, we shouldn't do it here or now."

10

LACEY

I trace his lower lip with my thumb. "You're good at that. Really good."

"At what?" He tugs playfully on my braid.

"Leaving me breathless. You did it to me at the airport too; ruining any chance for another guy to top that kiss." Not that I want to kiss another guy any time soon.

"Oops… Sorry about that." He smirks with satisfaction. "No, I'm not sorry. I had to know what it felt like to kiss the most beautiful woman I've ever met. I was dealing with something at the time—I still am—but you lifted the fog for a while. Anybody would be lucky to have you in their life. And I got you for a plane ride. And look how fate brought us together again."

"You really know how to impress a girl with those soft lips and slick lines."

"These lips?" His warm lips skim along my collarbone, making my body burst into flames more than the sunburn that I have. I let him tease me for a little while. He's testing my willpower, and I shiver.

"Your skin is so hot, but you're shivering. Is it your sunburn or me?" His breath tickles against my skin.

"We both know why I'm shivering." I wrap my arms around his shoulders as he grazes on my neck. "I still have your sweatshirt and lip balm. Now I know why your lips are so soft. Did you let me keep it, or did you forget it?"

"It was the last thing on my mind so, yes, it was an accident. But I did like how you looked wearing my clothes. Since I'm in the sun so much, I use sun protection everywhere, including my lips."

"I thought I'd never see you again after customs and suddenly, you were there. Then we left the airport, and I thought I'd lost you for sure, but your twin brother popped up. It's funny. When I saw Josh the first time, and I thought it was you, I didn't get that magnetic pull or charge. Something was off. Only when I saw you yesterday, before I fell in the water and was shocked by you having a twin, did it come back. I already knew which one was you just from that feeling, but I had to make sure."

He turns his head to expose his birthmark. "My parents used this to distinguish between the two of us when we were babies. I can't believe you noticed it so quickly."

"Well, my nose was practically rubbing against your ear on the plane." I press my lips against the mark, then trail kisses down his neck. His hands grip my hips again, but he behaves.

"So what do you do back home?" he asks. "I hardly know anything about you. Maybe I should've asked you more questions before I stole your breath away."

"Don't get too high on yourself, mister." I wiggle on his lap, and he growls. "I can feel how much your body reacts to mine—and I have the upper hand right now."

"Before you torture me any further, can you get up for a second, please?"

I move back and swing my leg over the side. My legs hurt from sitting in that position anyway. I stand up and shake the sand off my pants again.

Will moves the two chairs so they are side by side and the table is behind us. He reclines both to almost flat. The lanterns still glow bright enough for us to see each other.

"Here, come lie down next to me. Not on me, though. It'll be your fault if anything happens," he teases as we get comfortable. He opens his arm for me to slide in next to him. I rest my head on his chest and my hand on his stomach. His hand finds mine again. Would we be the couple who can't keep their hands off each other? Always holding hands, even just eating at a restaurant or going shopping? What the hell am I thinking? When would we ever be able to do any of that?

"So let's behave and answer the question. What do you do back in the city?"

"My sister-in-law is a dress designer. She has her own fashion label called JCD. I'm her assistant. We just moved into a bigger office space in Manhattan because her business is doing really well."

"Do you like your job?"

I hesitate.

"When you have to think about it, that's not a good sign."

He rubs my back, and I freeze. He lifts his hand.

"Sorry, my sunburn stings."

He moves his hand to my lower back. Much better. I can feel my skin getting worse.

"Anyway, I do like my job, but I don't know if it's what I want to do for the rest of my life." I explain to him what my job entails as an assistant and how much I love working with Jocelyn.

"If you had the chance to change your job or your life, what would you want to do?"

I sigh. "That's the problem; I have no idea. The one thing I do know is that I'd leave the city." We chat a while about what we like and dislike about living in a big city. He's lived in Boston and New York City.

"Are you happy with your job?" I ask. "How did you end up here when you were ready to play baseball? What made you change paths?"

He takes a deep breath. "Three weeks before Josh and I were supposed to graduate from college, our mom died."

My stomach turns. "Oh my gosh. What happened? Was she sick?"

"She told Dad that she fell and hit her head right before he got home from work. She said it hurt but she was fine. Well, she wasn't fine. She didn't wake up the next morning. She had a concussion and didn't know it. Just a freak accident."

I rub his chest gently. "I'm so sorry. I can't imagine what you went through."

"Thanks. My dad was a mess, of course. It was hard for Josh and me and our sister Chloe, because we were all away at school. He had to deal with it by himself before we could get there. I'll never forget the moment I saw him. He completely fell apart in front of us. I hadn't seen him like that before. He was always the strong one. Mom was the glue that kept us together.

"I decided right then that baseball wasn't my future. My family was. As soon as I made the decision, it was a relief. It showed me that I wasn't as serious as I thought I was about pursuing a baseball career."

He reaches for the bottles of water and hands me one. I take a drink, then listen to the sound of the crashing waves mixed with his heartbeat. I try to picture a younger Will, dealing with his mother's death. It breaks my heart.

"I know what you mean to an extent. I wanted to go to a college where it's warm and sunny all year round. I was accepted into a couple of them in Florida. But right before I was going to choose, my parents told us that they were getting a divorce. It was like a slap in the face. None of us even suspected that they weren't happy. I guess when I look back, I can see it. Anyway, instead of going to college in Florida, I stayed in the city to be with my brothers. Everything we knew changed."

"These big forks in the road pushed us in different directions, and look at where we are now. Together in St. Thomas."

I take another sip. "Amazing, isn't it?"

"Mmhmm." He kisses my forehead tenderly.

"Why were you so sad on the plane? You seem much better now." I roll onto my belly so I can see him when he talks.

His eyes close. "My best friend's wife, Deb, died less than a month ago. Josh and I were in New York to help Sawyer and to be there for the funeral. We all grew up together. It was never Sawyer *or* Deb. It was always Sawyer *and* Deb. They were a package deal. Now she's gone.

"She had a heart transplant when we were fifteen. Sawyer hadn't left her side since then. This time, she went in for a routine procedure, and her heart gave out. And I feel helpless because I'm so far away. Why couldn't it have happened during the second half of the year when we live in the Hamptons?"

"Wait a second." I push myself up and sit back on my knees. "Sorry. Not to change the subject, but… you don't live here all year round? I thought you worked here."

"I do. January thru June, Josh and I work down here. July thru December, we work in the Hamptons. We own a marina there too."

"You *own* this marina?" My voice squeaks.

I'm shocked when he tells me how he and Josh own part of the marina with their uncle. But he lives in the Hamptons six months out of the year. Maybe I could see him after this vacation. No, I shouldn't think past the last day of vacation or maybe even tonight.

"Does your uncle own the marina in the Hamptons too?"

"No. He owns a lot of hotels, including the Leonardo Grand in Manhattan."

"No way!" I smack his arm playfully. "I guess I should've put two and two together. That is a beautiful hotel. I've been to a couple of weddings there. My brother, Drew, just got engaged, and that's on their list of wedding reception possibilities. His fiancée, Sophia, loves it there. But who knows if a room will be available in such short notice."

"My cousin runs that hotel. Maybe I can connect your brother with him."

"That would be great. I love where it's located because it's near the flower district. One of my favorite florists is there. Every spring, I practically wait in line to buy the peonies. They're my favorite flower, my favorite scent. The store stocks every color possible, but I usually focus on the pink and white ones. Flowers are my passion, but it's too bad I have a little apartment with no balcony."

"That doesn't surprise me."

"What do you mean?"

"Well, pink hair, your shirt is pink, the tank top on the plane was pink. I think you have a pink fetish."

I lean over him and brace my hands on the sides of his head. My chest barely touches his. His hand finds exposed bare skin on my back between my shirt and pants. Heat rushes through my blood like liquid silk.

"Maybe I do, and that's why I find your pink lips so irresistible." I hover my mouth over his, but just when he's about to take the bait, I pull away.

"That's mean." He scowls but then a tempting grin follows. "They're not that irresistible if you can easily deny me like that."

"Oh, they are."

"Then show me." He draws circles on my bare skin, making me want to do more than kiss.

I refrain because I'm not usually so forward on a sexual level, but I slowly lower my head, my eyes never straying from his beautiful ones.

Until he licks his lips, and then all bets are off. My tongue slowly brushes his lower lip. Then I dip between his lips and his tongue greets mine with slow strokes.

And then this perfect moment is sadly interrupted by a group of people laughing as they walk past us on the boardwalk. I hide my face in the crook of his neck.

"So, back to the conversation. Which florist were you talking about?"

I sit back on my knees again. "Why?"

He tickles me. "Just answer the question."

"Blooming Beauties."

He laughs. "That's my sister's shop."

"You're lying!"

He shakes his head.

I push wisps of hair away from my face. "This is

hard to digest. Your sister, Chloe, owns my favorite florist. I suggested her store for the wedding too. If there's one thing I want to be involved with when it comes to the wedding, it's the flowers."

"Chloe creates all the floral arrangements for the hotel. She has one hell of a reputation for someone her age."

"It's kind of creepy that your family is connected to the same hotel and florist that might be used for my family's wedding."

"There's nothing creepy about it. It's just a coincidence." *Maybe.*

"All three of you have your own businesses. They sound like successful ones, and you're so young. I guess I shouldn't say that because I have no clue how old you are."

"Josh and I are thirty, and Chloe is twenty-eight."

"So you aren't too old for me," I joke. "I'm twenty-seven."

"Are you trying to say I look old, little lady?" He pulls me down next to him again.

"Of course not." I giggle, then kiss his cheek.

"Anyway, my mom had life insurance. Dad split it three ways. He's well off, so he wanted us to get the chance to do what we want. I had my MBA in advertising, but I had no desire to sit behind a desk. Josh didn't either. That's when my dad's friend approached us about the marina in the Hamptons. A couple of years later, my uncle made us an offer we couldn't resist for the marina here. Somehow, we worked it out with the six months here and six months there. So here we are. You say flowers are your passion—well, this is mine."

So many questions are popping up in my head, but I don't want to bombard him. I'm no stranger to the Hamptons, though, and I want to ask where the marina is.

"Excuse me." A deep voice startles both of us. "You're not supposed to be here during the night." A beefy man is standing a couple feet away from us. Security guard? He approaches us, and we can see his features in the lantern light.

Will stands up. "Hey, Stan. It's me, Will Mayes."

"Oh. Hi, Will. Good to see you." They shake hands. "Sorry to interrupt. Usually it's Josh who's out here."

Will laughs, but I don't because Josh is with Sky. He'd better behave with her. But Sky's a tough cookie. She can hold her own. But, wait. They could be doing what we were just doing.

They chat for a few minutes, and then Will introduces me to Stan, the security man.

"Anyway, you know the rules, Will. I'll give you a few minutes."

"I know, but—"

"It's okay, Will," I interrupt. "I really need to get back. I should check on Sky."

Stan walks away, and I help Will straighten the chairs. "You seem to be popular."

"We're like a big family here. This is part of my uncle's place, so we get away with stuff sometimes."

"It's nice to hear you haven't been caught doing this before."

He walks around the chair and places his hands on my hips. I wrap my arms around his waist and look up at him, ignoring the sting from my sunburn.

He nuzzles my hair. "That's because I've never *wanted* to be out here like this with anyone. I try to avoid getting involved with hotel guests."

"Aren't I a guest?"

"You aren't an ordinary guest." He kisses me gently. "You're the sweet girl I met on a plane. Things have changed since you showed up in my life… twice now. I haven't been involved with anyone in a while. It's too complicated with my living arrangements." He blows out two of the three lanterns but leaves one lit so we can see each other.

"So are things about to get complicated?"

"Maybe. I don't think a week with you will be enough."

I step out of the elevator and head toward my room like a zombie. Will walked with me to the lobby but had to leave because Sawyer called. It's sad how his face and mood changed when he saw Sawyer's name on the phone. He kind of closed himself off and said he had to go. Then he left without a kiss goodbye or an "I'll see you tomorrow."

We passed Josh on the way back to the hotel, and

he said Sky had gone back to the room. I hope she isn't sleeping, because I need to talk.

I slide the card into the lock and it clicks. The door swings open.

"There you are," Sky greets me, wearing her pjs and a towel twisted on her head. "I was starting to think you weren't coming back tonight."

I mosey through the door, but my mouth drops open when I see our room.

"Was there a hurricane in here but only over your bed? I don't remember you having so much stuff in your suitcase. And add that to the number of pillows on the bed. What a mess."

"Whatever, girl. I'm on vacation," Sky sasses. "Oh, man. Your sunburn. Does it hurt?" She presses my shoulder with her finger. "Your skin is so hot."

I search through my travel bag for some ibuprofen, then grab a water bottle and guzzle down two pills. A shower is next or maybe cool, wet towels. I plop onto my bouncy bed, which is nice and neat. "I wish I had skin like yours. My body's on fire but not just from the sunburn. Will is so adorable. I have *such* a crush."

"Now your smile looks like his from this morning."

"Yeah, but right when he walked me back to the hotel, his friend called. His mood changed instantly."

"Sawyer?"

I jerk my head back. "How did you know that?"

She tosses clothes over to one side of her bed, sits cross-legged, and hugs a pillow. "Josh told me about him and his wife. I can't even imagine how he feels. Josh thinks Will is taking it almost as hard as Sawyer. He says Will wears his emotions on his sleeve and takes on other people's problems as if they're his own. Being here in St. Thomas is a distraction for him, but when Sawyer calls, reality sets in."

"Yeah, when he answered just now, his face completely changed. One second, we were happy, making out like teenagers, and then, *bam*, gone. He just said he needed to go and left me standing there. But I can't be angry when I know why."

"Did Will tell you about their mom too?"

"Yes." I sigh. "That poor family."

"Two important women in his life died tragically. It's got to fuck with your head. And Sawyer's his best friend, so of course, he wants to be there for him whenever he calls."

"But Will made it sound like Josh is close to Sawyer too. They grew up together."

"Yeah, but it seems like he's the opposite of Will. Not that I know him that well… or at all. But it's almost like Josh faces it and it's done. It's life. He gets it out of his system and keeps going. That's the only way I can explain it when I listened to him describe what happened. I don't want to say he's cold. But maybe he hides his emotions like most men, and Will doesn't."

"It's amazing how identical twins can have such different personalities." I wave my hands in front of me. "But we're getting way ahead of ourselves. We've known them for like a day. So how long did you hang out with Josh? Did he behave?"

"I caught him staring at my boobs a couple times, and I smacked him upside the head. Then we just laughed it off. He's harmless. He's funny too. I didn't expect it."

"I'm surprised he told you all this when you just met."

"Well, I had to drill him a little bit about Will. Hello, my friend walked off with his brother. I had to know if he could be trusted."

"Is there any attraction there?"

Her head drops forward and the towel falls off. She looks up and ruffles her hair. "Nah. He's handsome, but that's about it. I got a brother kind of vibe from him. I think he felt it too. But he's great to have around because the crazy guys stayed away. We hung out in the lobby and analyzed people. He also told me they went to college in Boston, so that gave us something in common. But enough about me. I want all the juicy details about this crush. You're so smitten."

"Smitten is an understatement, and that's what scares the shit out of me."

Maybe I'm only meant to be his distraction this week. I'm good at making people happy. But will *I* be happy when I leave on Saturday?

Or will things get complicated, like Will said?

Yes.

11

WILL

I'm sitting at my favorite spot on the dock again with a cup of coffee, looking out at the tranquil turquoise water. I'm such a dick for leaving Lacey the way I did last night. As soon as Sawyer called, reality kicked in. I'm not on vacation like Lacey is. I have a life down here and other things going on back home. Sawyer keeps telling me I should never fall for anyone because they'll just be taken away from me. Why does that make me think of Lacey?

I keep thinking about Dad, too, and how hard it was for him to move on without Mom. He's only just started getting back into the dating scene after so many years. Is it worth it to love someone that much? Why am I even thinking about Lacey when I ask myself this question?

She's a good distraction for one week, that's all. A distraction who makes me horny as hell, though. I could've taken it further with her last night, but she's not the type and neither am I.

"Hey, bro." Josh sits down next to me. "You were up bright and early this morning. I didn't hear you come home last night or even leave this morning. Wait, *did* you come back last night? You sly dog." He punches me in the arm.

"I'm not in the mood, Josh. Sawyer called, and I left Lacey in the lobby to talk to him."

Josh moans. "Will, I know Sawyer is going through something that I hope we never have to experience, but you can't just drop everything for him. He needs to mourn, with or without you. I know you want to be a good friend, but you can't be there for him all the time. You're sad yourself; hell, we're all sad about what happened."

I give him a dirty look. "That's where we're different, Josh. You deal with these things for five minutes, and then you're good to go. I don't know how you do that. One of our best friends just died. Don't you think we should still be grieving?"

He shrugs.

"Well, I do. It only happened a couple weeks ago, not five years. If I'm the only one he feels he can talk to, then I'm going to be there for him."

"But every time you talk to him, you become miserable and a bit of an asshole. The only time you've been happy since we got back is when Lacey's around."

"We've been back for two days. She's fun to be around." *A beautiful distraction.*

"Then take advantage of her being here. Have a

little fun. Make *yourself* happy for once, then be miserable when she leaves."

"So no matter what, I'll be miserable."

"Only if you let yourself be."

"*Pfft.* Whatever."

I was stupid yesterday. Skylar came in to book a day cruise to Virgin Gorda and Jost Van Dyke in the British Virgin Islands, and I decided to make myself the captain and Josh a guide, even though we have tons of work to do. I figured this was my best bet if I didn't find Lacey last night. Now I'm not so sure it was a good idea. Our regular captain, Mike, was confused when I told him we were coming along today. I had to reassure him his job wasn't on the line.

This cruise is for ten people. One by one, people get on the boat. The two guys from the dance club last night are here. Is that a coincidence, or did they plan this? We're close to leaving, but Lacey and Skylar aren't here yet.

"Josh, did Lacey and Skylar cancel? They're late," I shout to him over the roaring of the engine.

"Not that I know of. Sky was looking forward to the trip when I was with her last night. Give them a few more minutes."

And that's what we did, and here they are, running toward the boat at the very last minute. Laughing and dropping shit along the way. Lacey's baseball cap flies off her head and almost falls in the water. I would never be bored with this woman.

She hops in front of me, out of breath, like she's landed on home base. "Howdy. Sorry we're late. The alarm didn't go off, and I wanted to run to the store in the hotel. Sky needed her coffee…" She babbles away with a big smile on her face. I feel myself relax again. "…But we're here now." She puts her baseball cap on backward. It might be the sexiest thing I've ever seen. I'm truly fucked.

I crack a smile. "You're the last ones. Hop aboard."

Skylar goes first, and Josh greets her. Lacey strokes my arm. "Thanks for last night. Will I see you later?"

"No." She frowns and takes a step back. I grab her hand and kiss the back of it. *Aha!* There's the electricity I didn't know I was missing. "Lucky for you and me, you'll see me all day. I'll be your captain and Josh, along with Mike, will be your tour guide."

"This day couldn't get any better." She smiles with delight.

I might have to agree with her.

"Hi," Lacey greets me from behind. "Can I hang out with you while you drive the boat? Josh said it'd be okay. I need a break from the sun."

I haven't seen her since we left the marina, but I've been hoping she'd find her way to me. "Sure. It sounds pretty rowdy down there."

She comes up on my left side, removes her cap and sunglasses, and places them on the helm. "Josh is hilarious. He knows how to entertain."

My eyes trace her beautiful, athletic body as she scopes out the cockpit. "This boat is gorgeous."

"Thanks. How's your sunburn?"

She focuses on me again. "Not good. I thought it would've gotten better overnight. No blisters, though. That's partly why we were late. I ran to the hotel shop to buy this bathing suit. This was the only one they had left." She's wearing a one-piece red suit with long sleeves and a zipper up the front. And it's zipped only halfway. Her hair is braided again, revealing her kiss-able neck. I picture her walking down the beach with a surfboard under her arm. Hot as fuck.

She tugs at the top. "It's a little snug, but I needed something that would give me more cleavage—I mean *coverage* today." She covers her mouth and we both chuckle. "I don't want to ruin my trip by having to stay inside all the time because I'm burnt to a crisp."

I pull her to my side, and she gasps. "You look sexy, no matter what you wear."

"Sexy, huh? You're making me blush." She pecks my lips, then steps away in regret. "I'm sorry. I have no control when I'm around you. After last night..." Her voice drifts off as her fingers trace her lips. "It feels so natural."

"I'm sorry for the way I left you in the lobby. I heard Sawyer's voice, and my good mood vanished." *Love sucks* repeats in my head from Sawyer, but I push it away. I keep one hand on the wheel and nuzzle her neck.

"Don't apologize. He's your friend and he's suffering." She caresses my cheek, then takes my sunglasses off my face. Her eyes lock on mine. "And so are you. I would've done the same thing."

How does this woman read me so well? "Thanks for understanding."

"No worries." She steps back and scans the helm. "You know, you're not the only one who knows their way around the Hamptons. I spent a lot of summers there, out in big motorboats like this one. So why don't you tell me all I need to know about driving one. Maybe the nautical world will be my next new passion." *I wish.* "What are all these buttons and different dials for?"

"We could be here a long time for that. I'll give you the very condensed version because we'll be at our first destination in about thirty minutes. You're going to love it. And then you can tell me about your time in the Hamptons. We'll see how well you know it there."

"You can test me later."

"What do I get when you answer a question wrong?"

She sidles up next to me, her chest rubbing against my arm. "A lot more of these." Her mouth closes in on mine, and my brain turns to mush. Once we part, I need a few seconds to see straight.

"I hope you fail."

12

LACEY

The Baths on Virgin Gorda are breathtaking. Massive, black granite boulders sprout out of the crystal azure water, forming tunnels, caverns, and pools to swim through and in. I think I've taken at least a hundred pictures today.

"Why did we book for only one week?" Sky says, sifting sand through her fingers.

"Because we'd be broke if we didn't."

"It's amazing, but I don't think I could live here. I'd go stir crazy after a while. I need my Dunks or Starbucks on every corner and the noise of the city."

"You'll get plenty of Dunkin' Donuts in New York. But you might think differently once you're there through a sticky, humid summer. But it can't be much different from Boston."

"Maybe."

We search through the shells where the shallow waves break on the sand. A large one catches my attention. I rinse it off. "Look, Sky. It's shaped like a heart."

"Cool. You can give it to Will when we leave on Saturday." She winks at me.

"Give me what?" Will asks, strutting toward us. I shove it in Sky's hand so he doesn't see it.

"Just a shell. I threw it back in the water."

I'd never get tired of looking at him. His sun-kissed skin emphasizes every toned muscle on his body. His angular cheeks and chiseled jaw are even more enticing today, but I don't know why. Maybe because I saw him mostly in the dark last night. Not in the bright sunlight. The golden highlights in his hair sparkle like sand in the sun. How is he still single?

"Can I steal Lacey for a little while?" he asks. "Mike is manning the boat until we have to leave. Would you mind, Sky?"

"Not at all. Where is everyone else?"

He points in the direction he came from. "By the dinghy bar, of course." We laugh.

"That's where you'll find me then. Have fun." She strolls off.

"Is this okay or would you rather hang out with the guys from last night?" He cocks his head, approaching me like I'm his prey.

"Is that a tinge of jealousy in your voice? Are you the type?" I walk backward in step with him.

"Not usually. But that one guy has been eyeing you up like a piece of candy."

"Well, I haven't noticed because my eyes have only been on you. And if he doesn't get it, oh well."

"Come with me." He reaches his hand out for mine. I twine my fingers with his.

We walk in silence until we reach a little secluded pool, hidden between some boulders. The water is a clear tanzanite blue. It's magical.

"Up for a swim?"

"With you, of course. With or without suits?" I flirt.

"Don't tempt me, Red. You're becoming my biggest weakness."

He helps me get past a patch of slippery rocks until we step down into soft sand. He wets his hands and drags them through his hair. Maybe it's not a good idea to be over here alone with him. I'm going to need arctic water to control myself. My weakness for him is becoming too powerful. Do I have to behave? *Hell no!*

He walks ahead of me, then submerges himself into the water. I follow slowly because I'm afraid there might be a dip somewhere. Eventually I make it over to him, and we swim around playfully.

"Watch out!" he yells and points at something.

I screech and swim away. "Was there a big fish?"

He bursts out laughing. "No. I just wanted to scare you."

"You're mean." I splash him the best I can.

"Well, there is a shark in the water and it's coming for you." He glides toward me, making the sound from *Jaws*.

"Oh, really. Sharks aren't the problem. I'm scared of guys named Will."

He stands in the water, but it comes up to his chest. He crooks his finger at me and flashes a wicked smile. At this point, I'll do whatever he wants.

Once I'm close enough, he wraps me in his arms. My legs have a mind of their own again, because they're already around his waist.

"Do you visit these places in your spare time? I can't imagine having all of this just a boat ride away."

"Sometimes. Mostly when family or friends visit or for business. I'm usually too busy running things in the background. Especially now, since we've been gone so long. I'm glad I have a team I can count on. This is not a normal day for me or Josh. We seldom run the cruises anymore."

"Why are you here if you're so busy?"

"Because of you, of course." He gives me an extra squeeze. "I wasn't sure I'd find you last night, so I figured the only other way would be to come on this trip."

My heart is in my throat when he says things like this to me. "That's a lot of effort for someone you hardly know and who'll only be here a week. Less than a week now. You could've canceled since you saw me last night."

"You said you have a lasso around your heart and it's connected to mine, right? Well, I feel it too. I'll take any amount of time with you. Work will always be here, but you won't be."

My heart is melting, and I know I'm falling for him. Is it real, or is it just because we're in this perfect, romantic place? Leaving on Saturday will be the hardest thing I'll ever have to do. But he lives in the Hamptons half the year.

Would I really want a relationship with someone who is only in the States six months out of the year? That wouldn't work for me.

"You've spaced out on me." He rubs his nose against mine. "I hope you're having fun."

"I'm having more than a great time. Want to know what my favorite part has been so far?"

"The dinghy bar?"

I shake my head.

"The snorkeling?"

I raise an eyebrow.

"I give up."

"Liar. You know exactly what I'm going to say." I rub up against him.

"Don't do that, or you're going to get in trouble."

"You mean this?" I do it again.

He pulls the collar of my suit to the side. He kisses and teases me with his tongue from behind my ear all the way down to the top of my breast. "Mmm, I like the way you taste with a dusting of salt on your skin."

I close my eyes and arch my neck to give him more access. He repeats the same thing on the other side. I'm so glad my sunburn is mostly on my back. I feel him hard against me, and I ache to rub more closely against him.

"I wish I could feel your body against mine. Skin to skin. No barriers," he purrs while he grazes on my chest. "Do you feel my heart pounding? I'm surprised it's not creating waves around us."

I run my fingers through his hair and stare into his hungry eyes. "What's happening between us? My heart and body aches for you. I almost can't control myself." I lick my lips. "Kiss me."

He brushes my lips gently with his. Our kiss is soft at first, savoring the moment. But a moan escapes from my throat, and we become more hurried and rough. He squeezes me against him like he fears I'll escape. I can hardly breathe, but I don't care. All I can think about is what it'd feel like to be naked against his delicious body.

Honk, honk!

Our mouths separate swiftly but not our bodies. His head drops to the curve of my neck while he pants and catches his breath. "That's our boat. It's time to go," he murmurs.

"I don't want to go." I nip his shoulder. "But I guess it's good timing before things got really out of hand. Not that I would've complained."

He unwraps my legs from his waist. "You drive me completely insane. Go ahead of me. I need a few minutes for a certain body part to calm down. You being next to me or even in sight won't let that happen."

"Didn't you know that's my goal? To drive you nuts." I giggle and swim backward. "You'll be begging me to leave on Saturday."

"Never. Now get out of here," he says, clenching his jaw.

I'm the happiest girl in the world... at least until Saturday.

13

WILL

"Thanks for taking this incredible day away from your duties," Lacey says. Everyone else has left the marina. Even Sky went back to the room, but Lacey stayed to help clean up and secure the boat.

"You're welcome. Thanks for your help just now. You're a natural. I'd love to see you again tonight, but I have to work. We're so backed up, and I have to prepare for a big meeting on Thursday afternoon. And some new boats are being delivered tomorrow… or maybe it's Wednesday?" I rub my eyebrows. "I can't keep the days straight."

"Then I'll stop taking up so much of your time. I'll head back to my room so you can work. I can't wait to get this suit off and shower."

I wrap my arm around her shoulder and hug her to my side. "I think you take pleasure in driving me batty. How am I supposed to work when I have an image of you naked in the shower?" I kiss her temple.

"Oops. Sorry." She giggles. It's the sweetest sound to my ears, but I prefer the moaning.

"No matter what, I'll find time. I'm not done with you yet."

"I hope not. You still need to test me on the Hamptons. Now go to work. Say goodbye to Josh for me." She waves and jogs off.

I cover my chest with my hand. It aches just watching her leave. What will happen on Saturday? *Love sucks, remember?*

I don't know how long I stand there, but Josh brings me back to the present. "Today better have been worth being away from the office. We have a ton of shit to do. We'll be here late, so I hope you didn't make plans."

I glance at him like he's an alien. "Who am I talking to? Have we switched bodies? I'm usually the one saying that to you."

"Well, Lacey's got your head so far up in the clouds, you can't see straight. Someone has to control things around here." He pokes fun.

We walk into the office and head to the back. I rub my hands over my face when I see the never-ending mess on my desk. It's true, my head is in the clouds... or maybe more like up my ass. We have so much work from when we were gone, and it has continued to pile up since we got back. I drop into my chair.

"I hope you know what you're doing," Josh comments.

"Huh? What am I doing?"

"I saw how you were with Lacey today. She's not just a week's worth of fun to you. She's more like a lifetime's worth."

"How could you see that when this is the first full day we've spent together? We're both adults; we're both attracted to each other. And we know it ends after this week."

"Who do you think you're talking to? I'm not Sawyer, I'm your twin." His thumb stabs his chest. "We have a bond that no one else has. I know when you're happy, sad, pissed, exhausted, scared, *constipated...* before you even do. You think I'm some guy who walks around not giving a shit, but that's where you're wrong. I see and feel everything you do; I just choose to deal with it differently."

I rest my elbows on my desk. "Where are you going with this?"

"She lives in New York City. We'll be in the Hamptons in a couple of months. You can see her when you're up there."

"And then what? I'd have to leave again in six months. That's why I don't get involved, because who'd want to deal with this lifestyle? No one wants to date someone who's only around six months out of the year. I just met her, Josh. Why do you act like I'm in love with her or something?" *You're close to it.* "You're the one who plays with them for a week and loves it when they leave. Why is that wrong for me?" I type in my laptop password with heavy fingers, trying to act casual when he knows he's annoying me.

"I haven't met someone I'd look at like you do her.

Even behind your sunglasses, I could see you watching her every move. And always with this lovesick grin on your face. Do you realize you two were constantly touching each other in some way today? Holding hands, thigh to thigh, lip to lip.

"Get my point, Will. I'm not saying it's wrong. She made you laugh more than I've seen in a long time. Why do you think I offered to drive the boat? If a stranger saw you two together, they'd think you were newlyweds."

"*Pfft.* Newlyweds. What the fuck are you smoking?"

"Come on. Even Sky sees it."

I stand up and lean over my desk. "Great. Now you're talking to Sky about us. What, are you best buds now?"

"Don't get so pissed off. All I'm saying is that it doesn't have to end when she leaves."

My brother, the gigolo, is giving me relationship advice. I must be on another planet.

14

LACEY

S ky stands in front of her messy bed with her hands propped on her hips. "I'm not going to be able to fit all these new clothes in my suitcase. I didn't realize there'd be such fantastic shopping here."

"I think we'll cry when we get our credit card bills next month. With the shopping, spa, water-skiing, and cruise, it won't feel like an all-inclusive resort anymore. I look forward to getting my bonus this month."

Yesterday was our spa day. We hung out in robes, had facials and massages, then relaxed by the pool for the rest of the day. I haven't seen Will or Josh anywhere. He did say they were busy, so I don't want to get in their way. I've been avoiding talking about him to Sky. This is our vacation, and I should enjoy it with or without a guy.

"How long are you going to stand there, staring at Will's sweatshirt?"

I avert my eyes from it. "Huh? What? I wasn't staring at it."

She crosses her arms. "*Okay*. How long are you going to stand there staring at the chair that's holding his sweatshirt?"

"Fine." I groan. "I was just wondering what Will's up to. It's Wednesday and I haven't seen him since Monday."

"Hmm. Let's remedy that. Send him a text?"

I hem and haw, then shake my head.

"I don't get it. Why are you so against texting him?" She rips a tag off a slinky sundress she bought today. "Oh! I've got it. Let's take him his sweatshirt."

There's an idea. He's always coming for me, so it's my turn to find him. I don't know why I'm so nervous. As soon as we see each other, we're inseparable. Why would today be any different?

"Do you know where he lives?"

"No clue."

"Then we'll go to the marina. Maybe we can convince Will and Josh to take us out tonight. Somewhere local."

"Really?" I beam. Jeez, I swear I'm like a teenager. "It wouldn't bother you to hang out with them again? Doesn't Josh cramp your style?"

"I told you, I'm not looking to hook up with anyone here. I had a blast on Monday. They're cool guys. It'd be fun to get out of the hotel one night. Maybe eat some local cuisine."

I check the time on my phone. "It's five thirty."

"I'm not going out looking like this." She looks me up and down. "And neither are you."

I glance at myself in the mirror. She's right. My hair is all over the place, and my smeared mascara makes me look like a football player. I probably stink too. Thankfully, I'm not cherry-red anymore.

"So let's hope they're still at the marina when we're ready, since you won't send him a message. If he's there, then it's meant to be. Just don't be disappointed if he's not or they can't go out."

No promises there.

I hate it that I'm nervous and my confidence is lacking. My palms are sweaty, and I have butterflies in my stomach. Sky told me to wear my black tank dress with black strappy sandals. Casual yet fun.

I slow down as we approach the office.

"No second thoughts! Let's go." Sky urges me forward. "It's now or never. He's going to light up like a firefly when you walk through the door. Guys only light up like that for me when they see my boobs."

I hip-check her because she's so ridiculous about her boobs. "Give me a break. And, no he won't. He's probably not even there." Just as I say this, the door opens and Josh walks out.

"Hey, beautiful ladies. Whatcha up to?"

"I came by to give Will his sweatshirt. He let me borrow it on the plane."

"Oh, yeah. He mentioned that the other day.

He's in the office. We're just about to close up. Go on in. I'll be right back. Want to come with me, Sky?"

"Um. Sure." They disappear into some sort of boat garage.

I knock on the door and then walk in. A bell rings overhead, and I cringe. Nothing like announcing I'm here.

"That was qui—" Will walks out of a room pulling a white polo shirt over his head. His abs flex with every movement. My mouth waters. He's so gorgeous. Once it's on, he does a double take and his face lights up, just like Sky said it would. "Lacey! Sorry about that."

"I'm not. That was a mighty fine view. Here's one sweatshirt and one 30 SPF lip balm." I lay the sweatshirt on the counter and secure the tube on it so it doesn't roll away. "I thought I'd drop it off… see if someone lost it the other day."

He walks around the counter and approaches me. "I think I know whose they are. You look beautiful as always." He cups my face with such care and teases my lips with his. "I've been thinking about you. It feels like a week since I saw you last."

And just like that, all my worries melt away.

I rest my hands on his hips. "That's nice to hear. I've been thinking about you too. I had such a great time on Monday."

"So did I. Especially our private swim." He winks at me.

"Behave."

He lays his hand on the small of my back and urges me forward. "Let's go to my office."

"I hope we aren't interrupting anything. Josh said you were closing up for the night."

"Oh, Sky's here too?"

"She went off with Josh somewhere."

"They'll be back in a minute. Let me send this last email." He pulls a chair over to his desk. "Take a seat."

"Sure."

I like the way he dresses. Nothing special—just basic cargo pants that emphasize his sexy ass, a polo shirt with the Twin Anchors logo on the chest, and tennis sneakers without socks. He can dress casually like this every day. What a life. When he's in this office, he radiates confidence and professionalism. It's attractive that someone his age has such a successful business. It sounds successful, anyway. Looks that way too.

My eyes roam around his office. His desk is neatly organized—laptop, pen holder, stickies, golden anchor paperweight, some colored files, and of course, lip balm and sunscreen. This makes me happy, because I'm the same way. I have to be on top of things at all times with my job. Jocelyn would fire me if I weren't.

Hmm. I haven't even thought about work or home or the snow. Should I feel bad that I don't miss any of that?

"Is this Josh's desk?" I point to the one facing his. It looks like someone threw a stack of paper in the air and it landed on his desk.

"Yes. You can see who's organized and who's not. But mine looked like that yesterday too. I was here late last night to straighten it up."

"If Sky ever got together with Josh, I wouldn't want to see their house. You should see how messy Sky's side of the hotel room is. But I don't think there's any zing between them."

"Me neither."

I zone in on some pictures on the wall of a beautiful motorboat. Josh and Will are smiling like they won the lottery. "When was this picture taken?" I stand up and point at the frame.

Will turns around, and his face beams. "Last year. We bought a new motorboat, and that was the day we christened it. See the champagne bottle in my hand?" I step closer to it. "It's our personal boat. It's not for rent. We use it when family or friends visit or if we want to enjoy it ourselves. I'll have to show it to you before you leave."

Before I leave. Dread washes over me.

I point to another picture. "Wait a second! I know her. She works at your sister's florist shop."

"She *is* my sister, Chloe." He chuckles. "My parents adopted her when she was two. She was born in Cameroon, Africa."

"I can't believe I've spoken to your sister before. How crazy is that?" I swat him on the arm. "Her skin is such a gorgeous shade of milk chocolate."

His eyes lose their luster. "This is the last family picture we have before my mom died."

"Your mom was beautiful. Actually, your entire family is. You and Josh look like your dad."

The doorbell jangles, and I hear Sky and Josh laughing. They are always laughing about something. Josh walks into the office, and Sky leans against the doorframe.

"Want to go to Crabscape tonight? We have nothing in the fridge. Sky's up for it."

"Do you like crabs or other seafood?" Will asks me. "Have you tried conch fritters yet? Not from the hotel. The food is decent there, but you need to try it at a real restaurant."

"Conch fritters?" I crinkle my nose. "They don't sound appetizing at all."

"You know those big shells that people put to their ears, thinking they'll hear the ocean? I'm sure you did it when you were a little kid. Those are conch shells," Josh explains.

"I know what they are, I just didn't know something lived inside them."

Josh laughs. "Yep. Tasty little critters. You can get them fried or with a delicious garlic butter sauce." He licks his lips. "My mouth waters just thinking about it."

"I love seafood. Let's go."

"I need to get out of the hotel one night while we're here. See what the nightlife is like," Skylar chimes in, swinging her hips.

"So let's get out of here," Will says.

❦

The sound of shells cracking and live music playing swirl through the breezy air. I have never seen so many crab legs in my life. It's kind of gross. The gigantic bowl in the middle of the table is almost empty now. There's another bowl to the side for the shells. All the tables around us on the busy restaurant terrace have the same setup. The guys are pros with the crab cracker. Me, not so much. I've sprayed myself with crab juice several times already, breaking mine. I'm going to reek of fish later.

"Are we ready for another round of Bushwackers?" Will asks.

I hold up my hand and finish chewing what's in my mouth. "Not for me. I'm done." Will gives everyone wet wipes for our hands.

"Me." Skylar raises her hand. "This drink is so yummy. I'm going to look for it in Boston when I get back. I've seen them on drink menus here but always picked something else. The name doesn't sound very appetizing."

"Bet they won't taste as good as the ones down here," Josh teases.

"What do we want to do after this?" Will asks, cleaning his hands. "Want to go back to our place? It's at the hotel. We can light the firepit and sit outside. Or would you rather go to a bar or dancing?"

"If we can make Bushwackers at your place, I'm in. I'm too full to go dancing, even though I'm loving the live band here." Skylar pats her belly. "Is that okay with you, Lace?"

Why do I have a feeling she's going to get drunk tonight, if she isn't already.

"We can, but we have to pick up the ingredients at the store first," Will says.

"I'm game." I'm curious where he lives. Let's see if his house is as neat as his workspace. Maybe I'll find some more clues about the kind of guy he is. Maybe we can find some time to be alone. The days are going too fast.

"I'll get the bill," Josh offers, turning in his seat in search of the waitress.

Not too much later, we're sitting in front of the fire on their patio. Josh and Will are telling us stories about the stunts they pulled in high school, switching roles and other pranks. Sky and I are laughing so hard, we're crying. Their poor parents!

I've seen things like this in movies, but how can it happen in real life? I've only spent a couple of days with them, and I can't imagine not being able to tell them apart. Well, I guess it could work if they dress the same and never speak. It did happen the first time I saw Josh.

"How about one more pitcher of Bushwackers for the night?" Josh suggests and stands up.

Sky hops up too. "I'll come with you to give the lovebirds some time alone. You guys want any?" We both say no.

I move over and rest my head on Will's shoulder. He pulls me closer and I drape my legs over his. A couple of lanterns like the ones from the other night flicker on the table in front of us. The fire pit crackles and pops. It's so cozy and romantic. Why can't I stay here forever?

The bungalow is simple and adorable. It has two large bedrooms, two bathrooms, and a large open living room/kitchen area. The whole place is decorated in basic blues and grays like our hotel room. Maybe it was originally an apartment or suite from the hotel. It would make sense, since it's on the property.

It's perfect for two guys who live here part time. There aren't many personal touches like paintings or photographs on the walls. No bookshelves filled with books or even curtains on the windows. Just window blinds. The kitchen has a coffee pot, blender, and a microwave on the counter. There's a center island with stools but no kitchen table. It's pretty clean and orderly for two bachelors. Definitely needs a girl's touch.

The patio area is secluded and private with a line of orange flowering bushes. It has an awesome view of the beach—well, that's what the guys say, anyway. Maybe I'll get the chance to see it in the daytime before I leave.

The buzz of the blender blasts from the kitchen along with some music. Sky's giggling about something again. I didn't know she was such a giggler… but I've never seen her drink so much, either.

"I'm glad you stopped by the marina tonight," Will says.

I lift my head off his shoulder and gaze at him.

"You need to give me your phone number. I

could've gone to the hotel and left you a message, but I don't remember your last name." He grimaces. "I'm sorry. You'd think I'd remember, but you only said it once. I know it starts with a D."

"It's Devlin. Have you ever heard of a jewelry store called Devlin's Designs? It's in New York."

"No. Sorry. I'm not much of a jewelry person."

"It doesn't matter. It's my brother's jewelry store." I shrug. "You gave me your number, but I didn't want to bother you."

"That's right. You were supposed to send me that picture. Why didn't you? You need to send it before you leave so I have your phone number finally."

"Lots of reasons; questioning everything about us. When we're together like this, I have no doubts how we feel about each other. But when we're apart, I don't know if I should be the independent woman who waits for the guy to come to her or the aggressive one who goes after the guy. I guess I'm feeling aggressive tonight." I growl a little and kiss his cheek.

"I like aggressive. Should I tell you how I feel about you?" He leans over and showers my neck with kisses. "I love the way you smell… like flowers in the spring."

"Oh, you do, huh?" I tease. "I told you, I love peonies. That's the scent of my perfume."

"I noticed how you smelled on the plane. I was hooked. I'll never look at peonies the same again. Or an empty plane seat, or a Red Sox baseball cap, or a red bathing suit… get my point?"

"Mmhmm."

"I love how happy you always are," he murmurs. "It's intoxicating. I can't be in a bad mood when you're around. Our flight was proof. You cheered me right up.

"And… I love that you hate it when I wear sunglasses. You look at me like you can see right through me." He cups my cheek and his eyes connect with mine. "Maybe you can even read my mind."

"I can't help it. Your eyes are so beautiful. I need to see all of you. It's like a wall between us when you're wearing them. I also like to watch the gold specks in your eyes sparkle."

He tips his head and presses his lips against mine. *Ooooph.* My stomach suddenly swirls, then clenches— and it's not because of his yummy kisses. Maybe it's the way I'm sitting after eating so much or from laughing too hard. I change my position on the couch.

Where were we? I grip his shirt and pull him toward me. *Cramp.* I let go and lean back. *Clench. Ugh.*

Will's head flinches back slightly. "What's the matter?"

I hop off the couch. *Clench. Gurgle.* I bend over and cradle my stomach with my arm. He springs up.

"I—I don't feel well. I should go back to my room." *Swirl.*

I'm deathly afraid of throwing up. I've only done it once in elementary school, and I've been mental about it ever since. I can't hear it, see it, smell it. A wave of heat rushes through my body and beads of sweat form on my forehead. *Please, please, please, don't do this! Not in front of Will.*

"My stomach. Nauseous and cramping. I should—" *It's going to happen.* I run to the corner but not quite far enough. I throw up on the bushes and the patio. Again. And again.

"Josh!" Will shouts from behind me. "I need a bucket. Now!"

A hand rests on my back. I move out of reach. "Go away," I cry. My body vibrates and my stomach clenches again. *No! Not again.* My legs shake, and I have no energy to stand anymore. I brace myself against the edge of the house with my hand.

"Lacey, please let me get you to the bathroom. You're shaking. Here's a bucket." His voice expresses concern and pity. I hug the bucket with one arm as one of his arms wraps around my waist. I'm almost airborne.

"Holy shit, Lace," Sky exclaims as she runs out of the house. "Maybe it was the crab or that other thingy we ate."

Thanks, Sky. Bad choice of words, and I lose my stomach again. Will picks up the pace to the bathroom. He takes me into his bedroom and straight through to a connecting bathroom. He lowers me onto the floor in front of the toilet and puts the bucket in the bathtub.

I kneel down. Water runs somewhere. "Here's a damp towel, sweetie. Wipe off your face and mouth." Will rubs my back, but this time I don't push him away. I don't have the energy. I'm so humiliated and disgusted. Why would he want to be in the bathroom with me?

"Please leave me alone."

"Nope. Out of the question."

"I should go back to the hotel. You shouldn't have to deal with this." I try to stand but fall back down. "Where's Sky?"

"She and Josh just went to the hotel to get you clean clothes. They'll be back soon."

I hang my head low. Water runs again and he lays a cool compress on the back of my neck. It feels good. I take a deep breath and try to focus on it, but my stomach's still pissed and it happens again. *Fuck!*

"Will, I'm so scared! I hate this so much and it hurts. Why won't it stop?"

He wipes my mouth and pulls my hair back, then flushes the toilet. I can't believe he's doing this.

"Don't be scared. I'm here with you. I'm sure it's food poisoning. It has to come out for you to feel better."

"I'm so sorry," I whimper. "I'll leave as soon as I can stand."

"You're not going anywhere," he says firmly.

Why in front of him? The guy I've fallen for. He gasps next to me. *Did I just say that out loud?* Fuck it. I don't care. I've made an ass out of myself in front of him so many times already, and he's still here.

Why is he still here?

I don't know how long I've been kneeling in front of the toilet with my head propped on my arm. At one point, I remember someone cleaned the bathtub and then they left. My legs are numb, and all I want to do is sleep. At least my stomach feels empty and relieved.

A soft hand caresses my shoulder. "Lace, here's some water. Try to drink this." It's Sky.

"Hey. Thanks." I force my numb legs out from under me and drag myself with my arms a few feet away to rest my back against the bathtub. Pins and needles start to prick my legs. The glass shakes as I bring it to my mouth. I take a tiny sip and wait to see what happens.

Sky kneels in front of me and rubs my leg. "How are you feeling? I have a change of clothes, your pjs, and your toothbrush."

"I'm better, or at least this round is over. Hopefully the water will stay down. Can you give me a tissue, please?" She pulls three out of the box and hands them to me.

"Do you want to take a shower? Will says there are towels in the cabinet underneath the sink."

I shake my head, then blow my nose. "I don't have the energy, but I'd like to brush my teeth. Hopefully it won't make me sick. I *never* want to eat again."

"Me neither after I saw you act like that chick from the movie, *The Exorcist*. I was drunk before, but that sure as hell sobered me up."

A tiny snort escapes. "Where's Will? Hiding?"

"He's hosing off the patio."

I squeeze my eyes shut. "Is he mad? Does he want me to leave? He has to go to work tomorrow… or today. I have no idea what time it is."

"Absolutely not. They feel horrible for taking us to that restaurant."

"It's not their fault. It could've happened anywhere. But why did it have to be me? Are you guys okay?"

"We're fine. It only takes one piece of—"

I cover my ears. "Don't you dare say that word."

"Sorry! Sorry!"

My hands drop to my lap. "Are you sure he's not mad?"

"It's all good. Relax. I was pissed off at him at first—he wouldn't let me in the damn bathroom to help you. I mean, who the hell does he think he is? We exchanged a few heated words, but then it clicked. No man would act that protective if he didn't have strong feelings for you. I know you want to deny it, but it's true. You're both going to have to come to terms with it. And the clock is ticking." She taps an invisible watch on her wrist.

"I might have told him that I've fallen for him. I thought I said it to myself, but then he gasped, so maybe I said it out loud. Is a gasp a good thing or bad? I pretended like I didn't say it. He kept quiet and eventually left the bathroom." I pull my legs up to my chest and rest my chin on my knees.

"I wouldn't worry—he's already changed the sheets on his bed so you have a clean place to sleep. If he had any negative thoughts, he wouldn't have done that."

"Hell, no. I'm not sleeping here."

"Oh, yes, you are. You don't have the energy to

walk back to the room. Anyway, it's a hell of a lot better than sleeping in a hotel when you're like this. Don't worry—I'm not letting you stay here alone. I packed some stuff for the both of us."

She unzips a black duffel bag and pulls out my pjs and my travel case. "Your toothbrush and toothpaste are in there too. Do you want me to help you change?"

I shake my head and unzip the travel case. "I can do it. Just give me a few minutes alone." She nods and walks out, closing the door behind her. I hear mumbling through the door, but I don't care.

I crawl over to the sink and pull myself up, then look in the mirror. My eyes squeeze shut at the horror reflecting back at me. I've changed my mind. A shower is a must. This is the most mortifying thing that has happened to me.

How could he ever look at me the same again?

15

WILL

I turn off the water and inspect the soaked patio and bushes. Good enough for now. I coil the hose and place it in the corner. Sky's in the bathroom with Lacey right now, but the only thing I can think about is that she's fallen for me. Not falling, but *fallen*. That's the best thing I've ever heard, even at a horrible moment like this. She stilled after she said it. I don't know if she realized she said it out loud.

I want to wrap her up in my arms and take away the pain. But I know she won't let me. I wouldn't let her touch me either. My instinct to protect her was immediate and took me by surprise. At that moment, I realized, or maybe finally admitted to myself, that I have fallen for her too. I keep making excuses as to why I can't care for her so much or how ridiculous it is to feel this way about someone in such a short amount of time. But there are things in life I will never understand. Even Sawyer's constant negative comments about love didn't prevent me from falling. I have to tell her how I feel before she leaves. Where we take it from there, I have no idea. Could we handle being apart for so long?

I open the door to the house and head to the kitchen to wash my hands. Josh and Sky come around the corner from the hallway.

"How's she doing? Does she need anything?"

"She seems to be better, but she's completely spent. She said she didn't want to shower, but I hear it running. Hopefully that will make her feel better, or at least alive again. I can't believe she's the only one who got sick. She's worried that you might be upset."

"She's crazy. I'd do anything for her."

"Yeah, I think we've all figured that out. Maybe you should tell her that before it's too late. Hmm?" she encourages me, then turns and walks into the living room.

I clean the kitchen quickly to give Lacey some time alone, but it's been a while now. Instead of telling Sky to check on her, I go to my room instead. I put my ear to the door and hear nothing. A lump forms in my throat.

I tap on the door. "Lacey, are you okay?"

I hold the doorknob, waiting for her response. It's quiet. Not good. If she's naked, I don't care. I quietly open the door and find her sitting against the tub with wet hair and pajamas on. She looks up at me with droopy eyes, and I realize it's definitely my heart that has the lasso around it now, and she controls the rope.

Her face is pale and her shoulders sag like all her

energy has dried up. I kneel in front of her. "Sweetie, how's your stomach?"

She shrugs. "I think I'm okay now. I'm exhausted. How can something like this knock me out so badly?"

"I haven't had food poisoning, but I'm sure it's a normal reaction. Let me take you to my bed." She moves to get up, but I stop her with my hand.

I hook one arm under her legs and the other under her arms, then stand up. She's light as a feather. Her head rests on my chest. I squeeze us through the door and walk over to the bed. It's already prepared for her. I lay her down gently. She makes herself comfortable on her side and cuddles with the pillow. Her eyes are sleepy.

"I'm sorry," she mumbles.

I kneel down next to the bed and push the hair away from her face. "Stop saying that. Shit happens. All I want you to do is get some sleep—as much as you need. You'll feel better in the morning. My house is your house."

She cracks a smile and her eyes slowly close. "I like the way that sounds."

I skim her cheek with my finger. "Me too," I whisper.

Slowly her breathing becomes heavy like she's in a deep sleep. I stay and watch to make sure she is. Her beauty radiates even at a moment like this. She looks good in my bed, hugging my pillow, in this room, in my house. I take a deep breath and kiss her cheek, then tuck her in under the blanket.

"I've fallen for you too."

16

LACEY

My tongue is stuck to the top of my mouth. Did I suck on cotton balls all night? And the taste is awful. I roll over, and my back and stomach muscles contract in pain. My eyes shoot open, and I quickly realize I'm not in the hotel room. Everything from last night replays in my mind in fast forward. I pull the sheets over my face. It wasn't a dream.

It's tempting to lie here all day so I can enjoy the sun beaming through the window and the soft sea breeze drifting into the room. I love that the AC isn't on and the window is wide open. I can hear the waves crashing on the beach. I'll say it over and over again: This is the life.

Hiding in this bed isn't helping me because I have to pee really bad. I need to face Will at some point—I am in his house. It's wickedly quiet. Maybe he's not home, and I can sneak out of here.

I stretch, and my muscles scream again, but I force myself to sit up. No dizziness or nausea. I look around the bedroom for a clock of some sort, but my eyes zone in on one thing. There's a glass of water on the nightstand with a big note saying, '*Good morning. Drink Me.*' It's not Sky's handwriting. My chest bubbles with warmth. How can something so small and thoughtful make me almost burst into tears? *Because it's from Will.*

I swing my legs over the side of the bed. After a few deep breaths, I pick up the note and trace it with my finger. This is going home with me. The lukewarm water goes down without any major discomfort. I make my way to the bathroom as quiet as a mouse and close the door. To my surprise, the room is immaculate. I love that. Fresh dusty-blue towels rest on the edge of the bathtub, along with new bottles of body soap and shampoo for women. My handbag and the duffel bag are on the floor nearby. I wonder what they did with my dirty dress.

I turn my head toward the sink, and there's another note next to another glass of water. My smile is uncontrollable, and so are my feet because some-how, I'm now in front of the sink, staring at the note. *Brush your teeth, shower, do whatever you need to. No rush. Don't forget to drink more water.* I'm melting onto the floor like lava.

Every second that passes, I'm not as embarrassed anymore. These notes alone prove to me that he's not bothered by what happened last night. They just prove how much he cares about me. And that makes me fall for him even more. *Shit!* What if I did say it out loud last night? The cringe factor tries to creep in, but I block it. I was only telling the truth and, well, it didn't seem to scare him off.

My toothbrush and toothpaste stand in a glass cup not too far from his. He doesn't have anything on the sink other than hand soap. I look behind me like someone else might be in the bathroom before I open the mirror cabinet out of curiosity. Just the basics in there. I pick up a bottle of cologne and smell it. It's Will's scent. It was on his sweatshirt too. I memorize the name, then put it back and close the cabinet.

I decide to shower again. It'll feel good to have fresh clothes on. I'm still weak and a little shaky, but I know it's because I need something in my stomach other than water. Maybe I should stick to tea and crackers when I get back to the hotel.

There's still no sign of anybody being here. My phone says it's eleven. I can't believe I slept so late. I expected Sky or Will to knock on the bathroom door by now. But nothing. I pack my stuff, wipe down the sink, and hang the wet towel.

With the bags strapped over my shoulder, I grab the two glasses and head to the kitchen. "Will? Sky? Anybody home?" I don't recognize my voice. It's so raspy.

I walk around the corner and stop, almost dropping the glasses. Will is sitting at the island with his laptop, looking more handsome than ever. His face lights up when he sees me. I glance at the counter and there are a couple varieties of tea boxes and bags of crackers and pretzels.

The floodgates open. He runs to me and takes the

glasses and bags away. Then he curls his arms around me. "Lacey, are you still sick?"

I wrap my arms around his waist as tight as I can—which isn't a lot—and rest my head on his chest.

"Talk to me," he pleads.

"I don't know what to say. You're overloaded at work, but yet you're still here. You bought me tea and crackers when I just thought to myself that's what I needed. It's like you've read my mind. Then your little notes and buying me shampoo and soap... I could've gone back to my hotel last night, but you let me stay here." I lift my head, and our eyes lock.

"You amaze me with your thoughtfulness and kindness. No man has ever taken care of me like this. I'm usually the person doing it for others. You have no idea what this means to me. Thank you."

"You're welcome." I wipe the tears off her cheeks. "I'd do it again and again just to see you sleeping in my bed, using my shower, and walking into my kitchen in the morning. But not because you're sick—it's because I want you here."

She lifts up on the tips of her toes and pecks me lightly on the lips. "I don't want this week to end."

"Let's not talk about it then." I can't think about it. My heart will go with her when she leaves, and I don't know how I'll survive that. "Is your stomach ready for some tea, or would you rather drink water?"

She unwraps her arms from my waist and lifts up the different boxes of tea. "You really went and bought these for me?"

"Sky told me which ones you like. I bought them all." I fill up the electric water boiler that I bought this morning, then turn it on. I've never had to boil water for tea here before. I could have just used a pot, I guess.

Her hands fly to her forehead. "Wait, I'm so horrible! Where is Sky?"

"Don't worry. She knows I'm here with you. I went to the office earlier to pick up stuff to work on here and went to the store for your tea. I forgot to bring stuff for breakfast. She said we live like typical bachelors and have no food. I kicked her butt out and told her to take a break and eat at the hotel."

"I hope she doesn't mind that I'm still here. This isn't the way we planned to spend vacation. Actually this whole vacation has been nothing like I expected."

"I don't know… she had a sort of twinkle in her eye. I don't think she minded leaving you here. I think she knew it would make us happy, that it'd be good for both of us." I rub the back of my neck. "Am I making any sense?"

Probably not. It's like we're all walking on eggshells to avoid talking about what's going on between us. Josh and Sky know exactly how Lacey and I feel about each other. They're giving us time together because it will soon be up. Meanwhile, Lacey and I are too scared to admit it to each other.

"You make perfect sense. They're encouraging us to spend time together before we need to leave early Saturday."

Just as she finishes her sentence, the water boiler clicks. I take a mug out of the cabinet and set it on the counter. She opens the chamomile box and pulls out a packet.

"Oh my gosh! What about Josh? Didn't you say you had something important to do today? You mentioned something on Monday. You should be at work," she babbles worriedly.

"Hey, hey. Calm down." I rub her arms and kiss her forehead. "There are things in life that are more important than work. Josh and I are a team. He said he'd take care of everything. I have my laptop and phone here, so I can work from home until you're well enough to go back to the hotel."

"Why are you doing this for me? For someone you hardly know?"

I place her hand on my heart. "Remember that lasso you talked about?" She nods and looks at me with puppy dog eyes. "It's even tighter now."

"I know. Me too." She blinks back another tear. "You've done more than enough. Even though it was the worst thing ever, I'm so glad you were there. I felt safe."

"Good. I'm glad. Now drink your tea." I pat her on the butt.

"Yessir."

"What time is your flight, anyway?"

"I think it's eight in the morning. The hotel told us we need to leave around five thirty." Steam rises from her mug, and she dips the bag in the water.

"That early, huh?"

"Yeah," she says. "I'm dreading it so much."

I know how she feels. "So, do you want pretzels or crackers?"

"Probably both, but maybe just the pretzels first. Thanks."

I grab the bag and walk around the island. "Let's

sit outside. You can see the view Josh and I were bragging about last night."

She hugs the cup with her hands and cackles. "Oh, you mean right before I became the new star of *The Exorcist*."

I open the door to lead her out. "Stop it. It's over and done with. The patio hasn't been this clean in a long time, though."

She laughs but avoids looking over in the corner. Instead, she sets her tea on the table, then gazes out at the view. Her body relaxes and her face lights up. "Wow. It's even more beautiful than you described."

"I never said Josh and I were poets." I chortle.

"I didn't realize that this part of the hotel property is higher. The ocean is endless, the perfect shade of turquoise with the crests of the waves mixed in. Those perky palm trees leading down to the ocean, the colorful boats sailing by, and the sprinkle of little clouds in that crystal blue sky—it's like a picture-perfect postcard. It's heaven."

"Wow. Speaking of poets!"

She flicks her hair back. "*Right?* I'm not sure where that came from."

"Hey, speaking of boats… I have a question to ask you."

She bends over and picks up her tea. When she sits down next to me, I curl my arm around her. Her body snuggles up to mine where it belongs. As if this is our norm.

"So what did you want to ask me?" she says.

"Tomorrow's your last day here. I haven't had the

chance to show you our boat. Can I take you out on it to watch the sunset tomorrow night? We could leave midafternoon so I can work in the morning. That's if you're feeling a hundred percent by then. I don't want you to turn every shade of green."

She twists toward me and I see the light in her eyes again. "Seriously?"

"Of course. I want our last night together to be special. It's been hard for us to be alone for any length of time."

"I'd love to!"

"But only if you're healthy and you wear that red bathing suit. You're not allowed on the boat without it."

She cocks an eyebrow. "You liked that suit that much? Your wish is my command." Her voice is deep and sultry. "I promise to be better tomorrow. And I told you, I don't get seasick." Her face drops. "Oh wait, I have to talk to Sky first."

"Oh, she approves," Sky says as she steps out on the patio. "Of course you're going to ditch me on the last night of our vacation for this hottie next to you. I'd be pissed otherwise. I'll be fine on my own."

Lacey stands up and hugs Sky. "You're the best! I owe you big time."

"Ha! You can repay me when I crash at your place during the next months. You probably won't think I'm the best then." They laugh.

"I've come to check on you, Lace, and to see if you want to come back to the hotel with me. We have to take advantage of our last days here." She points at the stuff on the table. "Even if we only drink tea and eat pretzels. I'll pretend I'm drinking tea anyway. But, no more Bushwackers for me for a while."

"Sit for a few minutes. Let me finish my tea, and then we can go." Lacey pats my knee. "This hottie needs to get back to work. Josh is going to hate me if he doesn't already. I'm distracting Will."

I squeeze her hand. "In a good way, so don't worry about him. If anything, Josh is encouraging us just as much as Sky is."

"We're the evil conspirators." Sky taps her fingertips together.

"I wouldn't say evil, but you and Josh always have something up your sleeve; with all your giggling and whispering all the time. You are definitely trouble," Lacey points out.

"We're just curious how all of this'll pan out."

Me too.

"I threw some condoms in your bag just in case," Sky shouts as we leave the slip. "You'll thank me later."

Josh cracks up next to her. They wave, then Sky cups her hands to her mouth and calls, "Oh, and don't forget to set your alarm so you can get to the lobby on time tomorrow morning."

I'm going to kill her. I give her a dirty look and then smile at the people who are laughing on the boat adjacent to Will's. My suitcase is packed and ready, just in case the night does go in that direction. Something I've been fantasizing about since I met Will.

"Ready, lady in red?"

"More than ever. Let's get out of here. I've been counting down the minutes since you asked me yesterday."

"Relax over here by me and enjoy the view. Unfortunately with this time of the year, the sunset is early, not like in July."

I stroll over to the cockpit. There's a huge glass canopy over us with a large open sunroof. The weather is perfect, and there's hardly a cloud in the sky. I watch as Will carefully steers the boat out of the marina. He's shirtless, showing off his muscles, and today, he's wearing a baseball cap backwards. I could look at him all day long and never get bored. I can tell from the smile on his face how much he loves doing this. And he gets to do it for a living and for pleasure.

"You're so sexy standing there with your fingers wrapped around the steering wheel. I wish I were the wheel."

"Come here, Red."

I tilt my head. "I kind of like when you call me that. Maybe I'll have to add a little red to my hair instead of pink." I inch toward him playfully, but he catches me off guard and sandwiches me between the wheel and his front. My body bursts into flames, and it's not from the sun.

"Here, put your hands on the steering wheel." When I do, he places his over mine. "Now we're both driving the boat. You're my co-captain." He leans into my ear and says, "But don't you worry, I plan on my hands being all over *you* later."

"Are you trying to kill me?"

"Yup. I finally have you alone. Beware." He kisses below my ear. He's lucky we're occupied with this boat.

We drive like this for a while, and he tells me all about his time down here. I guess it's not always heaven when storms and hurricanes roll in. The same with the Hamptons. I lean my head against his chest and soak in the scenery. I should be taking pictures.

"Can I sneak away for a second? I want to grab my phone from my bag. It's too beautiful out here not to take pictures. I'll add them to my collection of at least three hundred." I laugh at myself.

"Sure. Do whatever you want. I know of a quiet place to anchor. Once we do, we can hang out and relax." He steps back to let me go, then pats me on the ass.

I go down to the cabin to get my phone. This boat is gorgeous and much more spacious than I realized. It has two bedrooms, a tiny bathroom with a shower, and a kitchen area with a table and bench to sit on. There's shiny wood trim throughout, and it's decorated with gray accents. There's plenty of natural light shining in the windows, so it doesn't feel cramped.

There's also a lounge area outside on the stern, with a cute table and large L-shaped bench that can be expanded into a bed.

My phone dings, and I take a minute to check my messages. I've been ignoring them most of the week. Drew, Sophia, and Jocelyn have all sent a bunch of texts saying how excited they are to see me when I get back and that I should send more pictures. One of Jocelyn's other assistants complained that she's overloaded and can't do everything herself. Like I really needed to get a message like that. Now she knows what I feel like when she's not there. Drew said the snow's almost gone and it should be warmer than when I left.

I should be excited to see my friends and family and to sleep in my own bed, but after one night in Will's bed (and he wasn't even there!), that's where I belong. It's crazy, but true.

The boat engine turns off. "What are you doing down there?" Will calls. "You'd better not be lying on that bed without me. Get your sexy butt back up here."

I grin but don't go up right away. This is what pure happiness feels like... but in less than twenty-four hours, I'll be back home filled with heartache.

"I'm back." I shade my eyes with my hand as soon as I'm outside again. When I can finally see, I'm speechless. "Will, it looks like we're the only ones on earth. There's not a boat in sight. The water looks like glass and everything's so still." I twirl around.

"We lucked out with the weather today." He comes up behind me and wraps his strong arms around my waist. "That's the way I want it—just you and me. Let's forget everything around us for as long as we can."

I twist in his arms. "What should we do first?" I play with the sprinkle of hair on his chest then trace the faint trail leading down to his abs with my fingertips. His muscles contract from my touch.

"I'd suggest a little skinny-dipping, but I like looking at you in that suit too much. How about snorkeling? We don't have much time until the sun starts to set, so let's take advantage of the light."

"Bring it on. When's the next time I'll have the chance to go snorkeling?"

"Hopefully sooner than you think."

I shrug. *If only*.

After snorkeling, Will brings out a tray of fresh fruit, assorted cheeses, and crackers.

"This is great." I kiss him on the cheek as we sit down. "I'm so glad I can eat again."

"I didn't bring alcohol because I'm driving. I didn't want you to think I wanted to get you drunk so I could take advantage of you," he says with an impish smile.

"I don't need alcohol, especially in the sun. I'd rather be drunk on you. Everything we've done today has been perfect. I wouldn't change a thing. You're so good to me." I rub noses with him instead of kissing him. I want to kiss him all the time. There's an urge there that doesn't stop. It's like he's wearing a big sign that says, *Kiss Me*. As we eat, his hand either rests on my thigh or holds mine.

After we eat and clean up, we change the bench outside into a bed. Will grabs a couple of pillows from one of the bedrooms. We cover the bed with clean beach towels because we still have our bathing suits on.

"Let's watch the sun go down," he suggests. "The colors are even more beautiful when you're out here. I love watching the sunset, but I have a feeling it'll be a completely different experience with you."

He lies down on the bed, then scoots over so I can

do the same. We stretch out on our backs next to each other, well, practically on top of each other.

As the sun goes down, the sky and clouds turn into a kaleidoscope of radiant colors. *Wow!* "You're right —this is the best way to watch it. I appreciate the beauty of it so much more." I turn my head toward him and realize that he's looking at me, not the sky.

"I love watching you. You probably don't realize all the times I've done it."

I cover my face and peek through two of my fingers. "Was I doing something embarrassing?"

"No." He chuckles and pulls my hands away from my face. "When we took the day cruise, I was fascinated by how you really enjoyed every minute. I watched you as you sat on the sand and aimed your face at the sun. You were right where you wanted to be… maybe where you belong. I also couldn't keep my eyes off this red bathing suit."

I flip to my side and prop my head on my hand. "Why are you so obsessed with this bathing suit? Is it because I look like I should be on *Baywatch*?"

He turns too, and we are only inches apart. "Good point. I did picture you more with a surfboard."

"That's something I haven't done before. And, since I'm a little accident prone, I should probably avoid that one."

"This is my favorite part… I've been dreaming about doing this." He holds the zipper and slowly pulls it all the way down, revealing my ample cleavage since I'm on my side. I push my shoulder back to reveal my skin a bit more, inviting him to explore. His eyes flare and then he gazes at me. My mouth goes dry, and my heart slams against my chest.

He dips his head between my breasts, then tugs the suit to one side, exposing me. I gasp and run my hands through his hair as he circles my nipple with his tongue. Our breathing increases. I want his lips and tongue all over my quivering, needy body.

I push him away gently and get up on my knees. First, I scan the area to be sure there aren't any other boats in sight. He props himself up on his elbows and his dilated eyes scream everything I'm thinking.

"Want to help me get out of this suit? You wanted me to wear it; now you have to take it off me."

He grins wolfishly and climbs off the bed. With my hand in his, he lures me to the edge. I lean against him. "Before we go any further, are you sure you want to do this? There's no pressure."

My hand strokes the bulge in his suit that's pressing against my stomach. "No pressure, huh?" I taunt. "I had a physical in January and was tested. I haven't been with anyone in a long time. If you've done the same, let's put Sky's present to use."

His Adam's apple bobs, and his eyes blaze. "I'm clean."

"Then let me get my bag." I trail kisses across his chest.

"Don't worry. I came prepared too. Give me a second. Don't swim away."

I won't swim away, but I'll fly away tomorrow

morning. For right now, though, I am one hundred percent his, and this night is only about us.

Once he's back, he captures my mouth with his while he slowly peels down the long sleeves, one at a time. His hands travel down my back and cup my ass under the suit. I place my hands on his shoulders. My swollen breasts rub against his chest, and it's like a match to a flame.

I lie back and raise my hips. He pulls my suit off, and I stretch my arms over my head, reveling in the moment. I feel so free and invigorated. In the middle of nowhere, stark naked, outside on a boat.

"You're so damn beautiful. The colors of the sky light up your skin. I wish I could take a picture of you. But memories will have to do."

He takes his time, kissing and licking, all the way up one side of my body. Goosebumps chase behind, and I've never been more turned on. My body moves by itself, encouraging him to explore more.

"Take your suit off," I purr. "I want your naked body against mine. Skin to skin. Remember when you said that?"

"Mmhmm." He opens a box nearby and pulls out a blanket. "Are you cold?"

"I will be if you don't get your naked ass over here." I pat the empty space next to me and he tosses the blanket on the end of the bed.

"Let's not waste any time then." He smirks.

19

WILL

I have so much I want to say to her; it's building up inside my chest. And now I'm kneeling next to her while she waits to give me the best farewell gift. I'm going to savor every second of every minute until she has to leave my arms for good.

My skin sizzles as it comes in contact with hers again. *Skin to skin.* Our mouths join and our hands explore. She arches her back and guides my hand between her legs. I hover over her. Her slick entrance tightens around my finger as I tease her petal-soft breasts with my lips. She groans, then grasps my forearm, encouraging me to go faster. Her wish is my command.

"My body and heart are yours. I can't—" she says between heavy breaths, driving me almost over the edge already.

I take my hand away and kneel, then grab a foil packet.

"Let me do it." She sits up and takes it from me

confidently, never breaking eye contact. It's a huge turn on. My heart is about to jump out of my chest.

She tears it open with shaking hands. "This is the first time I've done this, but you seem to bring out the devil in me."

"Stop talking," I groan. "If you don't, I'm going to finish before we even get started." A sweet giggle releases.

Once it's on, she takes my hands and pulls me with her as she lies back down. I position myself between her legs. Her hands roam down my chest to my abs, making every muscle in my body contract. I push slowly into her sweet warmth, trying to savor this moment, but my body takes over. Moans of delight release from Lacey's beautiful mouth. I prop my hands on the sides of her head and lock eyes with hers. And that's when I finally admit that I'm in love with her. Her eyes reflect every color of the sky and glisten with tears. Without looking away, I pump faster and she grabs my ass, pulling me in deeper.

"It feels so good. Don't stop!"

Noises I've never made before come from deep inside as I build up to the most powerful orgasm I've ever experienced.

"Will, I'm… I'm…" She cries out as she tightens around me, and I follow right after her. After a few quick breaths, I wrap her in my arms, not leaving her body. We stay this way, holding on to each other, afraid to lose our connection.

Finally, I unwrap myself to see her face, but she's looking the other way. I turn her face to me and see tears streaming down her cheeks. "How can I leave here... leave you... tomorrow? This was the most beautiful experience. Not just now, but this entire week. I want to be connected to you like this forever, but we can't. Tomorrow, everything goes back to normal and it crushes me. I'm not the same person I was when I first stepped on that plane," she sobs.

I dispose of the condom quickly and pull the blanket up over us. I curl up tight to her again, and she buries her face in the crook of my neck.

"Do we have to end after today?" I ask. "I'll be back in the States in July."

She leans away from me. "And then what? We continue and then you leave for six months again? It wouldn't be fair for either of us. Look at us after one week together."

"I know." I press my lips against her forehead. "I know."

She's right. Neither one of us can promise anything. We have different jobs, and mine puts me over fifteen hundred miles away from her every six months. I can't ask her to quit her job and come with me. I'm lucky because I have Josh. She'd have to leave her family.

I love her, but I'm not sure I should tell her. It would be selfish of me.

She takes a shaky breath. "I knew this day was coming, but I didn't expect this awful heartache, knowing you won't be on that plane with me tomorrow. You're part of me now, but I have no idea what to do with that. Was this a mistake?"

"No! We were meant to meet, Lacey. There's no other way to explain it. I don't want you to leave, but what choice do we have?"

She gazes up at me and wipes away a tear trailing down my face. I didn't realize I was crying too.

"Let's make the heartache go away and live only in this moment." She turns us so I'm on my back now and she's straddling me. I push up onto my elbows while she trails kisses from my pecs all the way up to the mark behind my ear. The pain in my heart is increasing, but it won't dull the love I have for her. I sit up and take her face in my hands.

"You own my heart, Lace. I will never give it to another woman." I kiss her until we almost can't breathe.

We make love over and over again, releasing every desperate emotion with every tear.

20

LACEY

I'm exhausted, but I can't sleep. Will's on his side facing me, sleeping peacefully. His chest is bare, and a white sheet covers the rest of him just below his belly button. It stirs my hormones again, if that is even possible after the number of hours we've just spent naked together. I let my eyes trace every line and curve of his face, trying desperately to fill my memory bank. I've got pictures of him on my camera, but that's not the same as the real thing. Tears form in my eyes again.

Eventually, we made it back to the marina, but we didn't leave the boat. Instead, we locked ourselves inside and talked for hours—when we weren't getting twisted in the sheets. We told each other things we've never told anyone else. Now here I am, staring at the time on my phone as if a bomb will go off any second. I set my alarm a while ago, but I've turned it off. We agreed that he'd come to the lobby with me to say goodbye, but I can't do it. As he is now, that's what

I want my last memory of him to be. Not me crying in his arms again.

I need to be thankful for my time with him and move on. Our lifestyles and jobs don't match. If I were to have him, I couldn't deal with him being around only part time. I'd never tell him to change his job, but heartbreak would set in every time he left.

My heart can handle only so much pain.

I move off the bed painstakingly slow. *Please don't wake up.* I stare at him one more time, then close the bedroom door. It's the right thing. I have to do it this way. I gather my things and stuff them in my backpack. I look around one more time to make sure I'm not forgetting anything.

My hands shake as I unlock the cabin door. My heart pounds; I'm afraid I won't get away before he wakes. Once I'm free and on the dock, I look back once more. The memories of us on the bed last night under the stars crack me open. I shake my head and run out of the marina. As tears stream down my face, I somehow text Sky and tell her I'm on my way to the lobby. She responds, telling me she's already checked us out and she's waiting for me.

I wipe the tears from my eyes with the back of my hand and push the hair away from my face. Sky won't believe that I'm okay. I don't know if I could fake it either. And I can't, because I break down when I see her.

"Holy shit," she says, hugging me tight. "I'm not going to ask you how it was because it's obvious."

"I just need to leave… now. I can't say goodbye," I hiccup.

"You didn't say goodbye?" Her voice rises, and the man behind the counter looks at us.

"Don't question me now. When does the bus leave?" I glance over my shoulder in the direction of the marina.

"In a few minutes. It's waiting outside."

"Let's go." I grab my suitcase and backpack and speed-walk to the bus.

My stomach turns from anxiety, thinking he'll show up any second. I know he'll be pissed off. I would be too. But I'm doing this for both of us. A clean break.

The bus pulls out, and Sky touches my arm. "Want to talk about it?"

Tears roll down my cheeks worse than before. This is it. It's final. I'll never see him again. I rest my head on her shoulder and tell her everything that happened last night. Well, not everything. She doesn't interrupt; she just listens. That's what I need right now, to release everything I'm thinking.

Once I'm silent for a few minutes, she says, "Do you regret meeting him?"

"No! Not at all! But it's not fair, Sky. This heartbreak… it hurts more than anything I've ever experienced."

"I still don't understand why you're so against seeing him when he's back in the Hamptons."

"I told you why. Six months out of the year won't work. What if things change in between now and then, then what? No, I just have to convince myself to look back at this week with a smile and think, *wow!* I'll let myself grieve until I walk out of JFK airport. Then it's business as usual."

Sky's face drips with pity. Her lips part as if she's going to say something, but then she doesn't. I'm not sure I want to know what she was going to say; she might make me realize what an asshole I'm being. I know I am, but I have to ignore that right now or I won't survive.

We find our gate, then I go off to the bathroom to change into my New York clothes. I don't go back to where Sky is when I'm done. Instead, I hide myself in a corner and take out my phone. I open WhatsApp and start a new message. For a minute, the blank space intimidates me, and then my fingers start typing away. I reread what I wrote a million times before I attach some pictures. My finger hovers over the send button.

"There you are," Sky exclaims, a few feet away from me.

Shit! I drop my phone on the ground, then quickly pick it up and stuff it into my bag. "I was just responding to some messages that I've been ignoring all week."

Has lying become my new hobby?

"They just announced that we're boarding soon. You were taking so long, I thought you might've gotten back on a bus to the hotel."

I have no energy to respond. My muscles are

beginning to scream from last night. It's a sweet ache I won't forget.

"Let's go."

≈

I collapse into the window seat, hug my backpack, and stare out the window. A part of me was hoping Will might show up at the airport. But why would he? We aren't in a Hollywood movie. I left him without saying goodbye. And what would it solve if he did? We just aren't meant to be. This was only supposed to be a hot vacation romance.

Why can't I turn around and look at the seat next to me and find Will sitting there again?

"Lace?" Definitely not Will's voice. "Can you send me that one picture of when I jumped off the boat on the day cruise? The one where I was midair. I've asked you a thousand times, but you keep forgetting. Or give me your phone, and I'll look for it."

I open my backpack and pull out my phone. "Scheisse!" I squeeze my eyes shut and bang the back of my head against the seat. "The screen shattered when I dropped it right before we got on the plane. I can't access anything." I want to cry all over again. I've dropped this phone a zillion times and it has never broken. But this time it did. Now I can't send Will that text message until I get a new phone.

"Shit, Sky! What if I've lost all of my pictures from vacation or all the ones of me and Will? I don't even have his phone number without it!" But why should I care if I've lost his contact info? My chest feels like there's a massive weight on it.

"Don't freak out. It's most likely only the screen. And you can transfer everything to a new phone."

"Great." I roll my eyes. "You know me. I'm technologically challenged."

"It's not difficult. If the people at the store you buy your new phone from can't help you, just call me. I'll walk you through it. And you never know, I might be crashing at your place next weekend."

I nod my head and toss my phone back in my bag. What I really want to do is throw it down the aisle at someone to release some of my anger.

"Do me a favor, Sky."

"Sure. What?"

"Don't tell anyone about Will. Especially my dad. The way he's so protective over me, he'll call my brothers and ask who the hell he is. Then they'll come to me asking why I didn't tell them about him. I can't deal. It's nobody's business."

"Whatever you want," she says doubtfully, "but I don't think you have to let him go like he never existed. You're going to completely remove Will from the details of our vacation?"

"I'll say we met a lot of people or something like that. Or I'll avoid the questions all together."

"Your family is going to see right through you just like I can. And they see you more often."

"I'll be fine once I'm back at work and have my normal rhythm. I'll be distracted. My smiling self will be back on display."

Right. Back to the chaos of New York. I just need time to get back into the New York state of mind. Except that's not who I am anymore.

Minutes later we're in the air and keep to ourselves, but my brain won't shut off. Sky has earphones in and reads her Kindle.

I tap her arm. She pulls her earbuds out. "What's up?"

"I feel horrible. Did I ruin your vacation? Did I make it all about me and Will?"

She hesitates. "In a way it was about you and Will, but I loved it. Watching your love story evolve was better than watching a movie. You were so happy—how could I not be happy? And Will is a catch. I just wish it could've worked out for you both. Things happen for a reason, Lace, like him getting my empty seat."

I don't know if she's trying to make me feel bad that I left Will without saying goodbye or if this is her sneaky way of getting me to want to see him again.

"But," she whispers, "my favorite part about this entire trip is that we've become closer friends and sisters. And I'm not going to use the ugly word *step*."

"Me too." I give her a big hug. "Next time I see you, I promise I'll be back to my old self."

"Is that what you want?" she asks gently. "Because I'm not sure you're the same person you were before the trip."

I know I'm not.

W hy is it so bright in here? I reach my arm out to touch Lacey but all I find are cold sheets. I bolt up into the sitting position and shout, "Lace!" *Crickets.*

I hop off the bed and search the boat. "Lacey, where are you?" All her things are gone.

Every hair on my body stands on end. "No, no, no." I yank my clothes on and burst through the cabin door. I slam into Josh.

"Where's Lacey? Have you seen her?"

"No. They left over an hour ago. Didn't you see her before she left?"

I pull my hands through my hair, almost pulling it out. "She didn't wake me. Her alarm was set, but I didn't hear anything. How could she have left without saying goodbye? How?" I shout at Josh.

He steps back. "Will, I'm sorry. I don't know what to say. I got a message from Sky, saying they made it to the airport okay."

My head perks up. My phone! I run back to the cabin and search for it. I snatch it off the counter and unlock it. A message pops up with a number I don't recognize. My hand shakes when I click on it. *Please be Lacey.*

"Did she leave you a message?" I ignore him and read:

Dear Will,

I'm sorry I left without saying goodbye. I didn't do it to hurt you but to save us. I wouldn't have been able to walk away from you for the last time. Thank you for the most magical week of my life. Last night will live in my heart and soul forever. Attached are some pictures of us. You will always hold the lasso around my heart.

Love, Lacey

I flip through the pictures and stop on one. She finally sent me the picture of her from the plane.

"Is it from her?"

"Mmhmm." I sit down on the bench and hand Josh my phone for him to read it. On the counter near where my phone was is a heart-shaped shell. I pick it up and trace it with my finger.

So many emotions are zipping through my body that I don't know what to think. I'm mad at myself that I didn't wake up or hear her before she left. I'm mad at her because she left without saying a word. But we said all we needed to say last night.

"I'm sorry, bro. What are you going to do?"

I rub my hands up and down my face. "What can I do? She's gone and not coming back. We knew it was only for a week but… I never thought it would hurt this bad. If it hurts like this for me after one week, I can't imagine what Sawyer feels like after losing Deb."

"Didn't you talk about seeing each other when you return to the Hamptons?"

I tell Josh what we said last night. "I understand what she means. What kind of relationship could we have? I don't want her for only six months." I growl and stand up. "But how can I even think that after only being with her for a week? Have I lost my fucking mind? How can such a beautiful woman get under my skin so quickly that I can't bear a day without seeing her beaming face or hearing her laugh?"

"I'm sorry it worked out this way. Maybe—"

"No maybes. She's gone, and I have to accept that. She's the one I want, but she's right. She doesn't deserve fifty percent. She deserves all of me. We both do. But again, how did we get to this point in such a short amount of time?"

"I'm not going to answer that for you. You already know why." He claps me on the shoulder. "I'll leave you alone. Let me know if you need something."

"Thanks. I'm going to clean up the boat. When I'm done here, I'll go to the office. I know it's a busy day. Thanks for covering for me so much this week."

"You bet. It was great to see you relax and have fun. It's been a while. I hope it was worth it."

"She's worth everything to me. I'd do it again in a heartbeat."

"Then take some time and think about what is right for you. If you care for her as much as you think you do, then do something about it. Maybe respond to that text or call her."

I nod.

If it were only that easy.

22

LACEY

I didn't tell my family about Will, and Sky has kept her promise and stayed quiet too. She's been coming to the city almost every weekend and has been getting to know the rest of the family better. Just like I told her, Jocelyn has welcomed her in like she's always been here.

Sky and I agreed on the same story to tell them about our vacation. We said it was awesome and we'd go back in a heartbeat. I managed to plaster my usual smile on my face before we got back, but it hurts to fake it all the time. It's exhausting to act like the peppy, positive one when I'm not anymore. And I miss feeling that way. Sky knows I'm still hurting, so she lets me talk her ear off most of the time.

I got a new phone, and I almost passed out when I saw that I'd somehow managed to send the text message I created for Will. I must have hit the send button right before I dropped the phone. But that hurt even more, because he didn't respond. Not even an emoji. But what did I expect? He's doing exactly what we agreed to do.

Meanwhile, I've become a bit of an online stalker —I stare at his name on WhatsApp and wonder what he's doing when it says he's online. I also looked up the marinas' websites, but there aren't many pictures of him on them. I researched how to get a boating license—and I don't have a boat!

I've walked past Chloe's flower shop several times. I've even stopped a few times. But as soon as I get hold of the door handle, ready to go in and introduce myself to her, I chicken out and leave. The peonies are there, and they're gorgeous, but I haven't bought any. My desire to buy flowers has disappeared.

To torture myself even more, I had a few red streaks put in my hair. My family and friends commented on it because it's not my usual color and it's more dramatic. They act like I dyed my hair completely red.

But today is going to be the test. Sophia and Drew have finally set their wedding date for the last weekend of October. They were able to reserve a banquet hall at the Leonardo Grand, Will's uncle's hotel. She set up an appointment with Chloe to discuss wedding flowers. She asked me and Jocelyn to go with her. I don't know how much more torture I can endure.

Chloe might recognize me as a customer, but she won't know who I am. Knowing that she's Will's sister kills me for some reason. I wonder if he told her about me and how much I love her flowers. Or does only Josh know about me? If I didn't tell my family, why should Will?

Wake up and smell the peonies, Lacey!

I want to smack myself senseless. It was vacation, and it's over. It was only a vacation romance. So why, after all these weeks, do I still miss him so much?

"There you are!" Sophia says. "We thought you weren't coming."

"I'm a couple of minutes late. You could've gone in already."

"We were having fun looking at all the different flowers out here. I love spring flowers. I understand why you gush over the peonies," Jocelyn says. "Too bad the wedding's in October. I'm not sure you can get them at that time of year."

"Chloe's probably going to hate me because I don't have a clue what I'm looking for. But she was super nice on the phone, and I'm sure she's dealt with worse." Sophia giggles excitedly. "Let's go in."

My stomach ties itself into knots, my heart beats like a massive drum, and my earlobes are hot. Why am I so afraid to meet her? Because she's the closest thing to Will I'll ever get.

They open the door and chimes ring overhead. A couple of other customers stand at the register. Sophia and Jocelyn go straight over and mention they have an appointment.

Chloe walks out from the back, and I go into panic mode. I freeze. If this is what an anxiety attack feels like, it's horrible. I watch as they introduce themselves, and then Sophia turns toward me.

"Come on, Lacey." She waves me over.

Chloe looks at me, and her eyes flash. She cocks her head slightly—or maybe I just imagined all of that. *I can't.*

I look away and walk out of the store. I stop on the sidewalk and face-palm myself a couple times. What the hell am I doing? I have got to wake the fuck up! The weight of not telling my family about Will and faking my happiness is weighing on my chest to the point I can hardly breathe.

"Lacey?" Jocelyn says from behind me. I turn to face her. "What's the matter? You're pale as a ghost."

"I don't feel well. I think I should just go home. Tell Sophia I'm sorry." I look everywhere except her face.

"Are you sure you can go alone? Should I take you?"

"No. I'll be fine. I probably just need to sleep a little bit. Sky should be at the apartment soon. I'll talk to you tomorrow, or I'll see you at work on Monday." I turn away and don't wait for her to respond.

"Thanks for listening. *Again.* I know it's getting old," I admit to Sky. "More wine?"

She covers her glass and shakes her head. I put the bottle on the table next to my phone. I've turned it off because Sophia has been calling for an hour. I sent her a text saying I'm fine, but she won't give up. Drew even tried to call. What's the big deal?

"Can I ask you a question?" Sky asks, twirling her hair. I nod.

"What will it take to make you happy again? Because nothing seems to be working."

Good question. I fantasize that he'll show up and tell me he's going to live in the Hamptons all year round. Other than that, I have no idea what I'm supposed to do. Should I start over somewhere new where nothing reminds me of him? That's a bit drastic. Running won't solve anything.

I open my mouth to say something, but someone knocks on my apartment door. It's probably my neighbor who's always asking for eggs or milk. I look through the peephole, and my stomach drops. It's Jocelyn and Sophia. I take a deep breath, then unlock the door and open it. Both of them glower at me.

They burst into the apartment and say hi to Sky. Then Jocelyn whips around and points her finger at me.

"You are going to tell us right now what is going on with you. Ever since you came back from vacation, you've been walking around with a fake smile, pretending life is a basket of roses. But you aren't fooling us."

"That sparkle that you've had ever since I met you is gone," Sophia adds. "You hardly talk about your vacation. Actually, neither of you do. Did something bad happen?"

Jocelyn interrupts, her eyes blazing. "Did someone do something to you?" I almost laugh. She's the sweetest woman, and you'd think she'd never hurt a fly, but she'd go to battle if anyone hurt her family or friends. She's badass like that.

"No, no." I wave my hands in front of me. "It's nothing like that."

"And!" Sophia raises her hand. "How does Chloe know who you are? She says you know her brothers. Why didn't you tell us that?"

Will told her about me. She did recognize me. Maybe he showed her one of the pictures I sent him.

"Oh, shit," Sky mumbles.

Jocelyn glances at Sky. "Why would you say that?"

Sky's eyes bulge. "Say what?"

Jocelyn sneers at her.

"What aren't you telling us? You're freaking us out!" Sophia exclaims.

"It's nothing bad. No one did anything wrong."

"Then why not just tell us? We're your friends and family. You're the light of this family, Lacey, only you aren't shining like you used to."

"For fuck's sake, would you please tell them about Will! I can't take it anymore," Sky demands, surprising us all.

Sophia's and Jocelyn's heads whip toward me. "Who the hell is Will?" they say in unison. This is actually kind of funny.

"Fine," I growl. "Sky, clear your stuff off the couch so they can sit down. I'm going to grab some glasses and another bottle of wine." And some tissues.

"Of course. Sorry." She grabs the shirts and jeans that are scattered over the couch and dumps them in a corner.

The kitchen isn't far away, but they start whispering as if I can't hear them. They're pressuring Sky for info.

"Here's some wine. Help yourself. I only have one bottle left." I place the glasses and wine on the coffee table, then pull up a chair from the kitchen.

Jocelyn and Sophia perch on the edge of the couch like they're waiting for the ball to drop. Sky relaxes into the couch like she's watching a movie. All she needs is popcorn.

"I haven't actually formally met Chloe, other than we've talked a few times when I visited her store in the past. No names were exchanged. But Sky and I have met her twin brothers, Will and Josh, on vacation. Chloe is their adopted sister."

"Twins? She didn't tell us their names either," Sophia remarks. "She really didn't say much at all."

I shrug, then, for the next hour, I tell them everything I can remember about Will. Sky chimes in whenever I skip some detail. It's interesting to hear things from her perspective compared to mine. By the time I'm done, my face is covered in a salt mask from all the tears I've shed.

"I keep asking myself how I can feel so strongly for someone I knew for a week. And I *still* feel that way now. It's fucking crazy." I pull my hair back with a hair band.

"You're in love with him, Lace," Jocelyn says matter-of-factly.

"Whatever." *I am.*

"You do know who you're talking to, right?"

Jocelyn says. "Your brother said he was going to marry me on our first date. And you're the one who set us up."

"And within weeks, well, days after we met, Drew and I admitted we were in love. And you helped us along the way," Sophia adds. "Now, four months later, we're already engaged. Love at first sight is real. It happens every day. Why can't it happen to you?"

"It's the only reason I can think of to explain how devastated you are," Jocelyn adds. "Why didn't you tell us?"

I rub my thighs. "At this point, I don't even remember. Maybe I thought it was the only way to forget him. I thought, if I didn't talk about him, it might be easier."

"How did that work out for ya?" Sky jabs with a twang of her Boston accent.

"But me dumping this on everyone doesn't solve anything. He's there, and I'm up here."

"So what. Would you ever consider joining him in St. Thomas?" Jocelyn asks carefully.

"And give up my job? And my apartment?"

"Yes," she responds firmly and crosses her arms.

"Are you crazy?" But I can't look at them because I'm suddenly excited about the possibility.

"Why couldn't you? You're still young. Your brothers and I have always said you're meant for the tropics, not the metropolis. This is your chance."

"We didn't even discuss that. It's too soon to talk about such a big leap."

"Let's say you somehow get together, and it

doesn't work out. You can come back—you will *always* have a job with my company. You're safe either way. With his job, he owns those marinas. It's not as simple for him."

"But I haven't spoken to him at all. I sent him that text, and he didn't respond. We could be talking about this for no reason."

Sky smacks the table and stands up. Jocelyn and Sophia almost leap from the couch. I think they forgot she was here. "Can you please stop making fucking excuses? You're scared shitless, and it's okay to be. But I saw you both, up front and personal. You've got the real thing, Lacey. Who cares how crazy it sounds? Not everyone finds their soul mate. You have."

She grabs her phone and her wallet off the table. "And on that note," she continues, "I'm going for a wine run. I'll be back in a little while."

She walks briskly out the door, slamming it behind her. Somehow, it's like all the air went with her.

Then Jocelyn motions to the door. "Yeah! What she said!"

For the first time since I left St. Thomas, a real smile grows on my face.

23

WILL

Three weeks have gone by. Every single day since, I have read Lacey's text at least once. I stare at the pictures on my phone. I dream about her at night like we were back on the boat again. Together. I miss her just as much as I did the day she left, if not more. I didn't respond to her text because… well, it would've just tortured both of us. We had our perfect night, and I'm not going to ruin the memories of it.

"Anybody up for a cigar?" I know that voice.

My head snaps up, and there's Sawyer walking toward me across the patio.

"What the hell are you doing here?" We clap each other on the back.

"I needed a change of scenery, and I know I'm always welcome with you two."

"Wow, I can't believe you're here. You look great. A lot better than the last time I saw you."

"I finally showered and shaved," he jokes.

"Come inside. You want a beer or something else to drink?"

"I'll take a beer, but let's sit outside so we can smoke this cigar I brought. Or I can."

"Sounds good. I'll be right back."

I'm amazed that he's here. He hasn't been calling as much anymore. Of course, I've been lost in my own head, so I haven't been the best person to be asking for advice. I take two beers out of the fridge and pop the caps off.

Sawyer's on the patio gazing out across the water, surrounded by cigar smoke. I only smoke cigars on random occasions. This is not one of them.

He turns toward me. "Deb sure loved it here."

"Yeah. We had some good times with you two." I hand him his beer, and we clink our bottles together. "How long can you stay? What about your job?"

He puffs on his cigar and exhales. "I've been doing a lot of soul searching. I went back to work, but I couldn't focus on anything. I got tired of everyone walking on eggshells around me and asking how I was doing. I wanted to scream, 'I feel like shit! Piss off.' Finally, I talked to my boss, and we both agreed I should take a leave of absence. It's only for a month. I need to figure out who I am without Deb."

"Are you going to stay down here the whole time?"

He shrugs. "No idea. As I said… soul searching."

"You're different in a better way."

"Meh. I have a few good days in between the shitty ones. Don't let looks fool you. But I had an epiphany. Deb chose to love me her entire life. *Me.*" He points to his chest. "Do you know how lucky I was to have her in my life? So, maybe instead of crying over her being gone, I should be happy that I had her for as long as I did. We were aware of her heart issues, and we were happy to be together every day. Her life was cut too soon, but we knew it could happen."

"As you've been saying, life and love suck." I sit on one of the couches.

He shakes his head. "Don't listen to me. I was in mourning. I still am. For a while, I hated everyone and everything. Deb was the only love I knew, and she was taken away from me. But I have to tell you, I was wrong about some things."

"Like what?"

He walks toward me but remains standing. "Love doesn't suck. I would never, ever regret loving Deb— even though it's killing me now. She lit me up inside and gave me so much while she was on this earth. We were the definition of soul mates. I knew I loved her the first day I saw her swinging on a swing in elementary school. *Elementary school!*"

"Yeah, I remember. You were like a little puppy, running around behind her during recess." I smile at the memory.

"So love doesn't suck. It's the best feeling in the world, but it can hurt like a bitch sometimes too. I don't know if I'll ever love another woman like Deb. It's hard to believe that could happen again. But I'd tell anyone to hold onto it if they found it."

Why is he telling me this? Can he read my mind? I haven't told him about Lacey. It didn't feel right.

"Why didn't you tell me you were coming?"

"Josh knew," he mumbles, then glances over my shoulder.

"What? Why didn't he tell me?"

"I wanted to surprise you. He told me about Lacey and how you've been having a hard time lately."

"He what?" Anger bubbles in my chest. "It's nothing compared to what you're going through. So that's what this speech was about? Look, it's nothing I can't handle."

"Not according to Josh."

I stand up. "What the fuck?"

"I needed someone to talk sense into you since you won't listen to me." I swing around. Josh is there.

"And what sense would that be?"

"To get your ass up to New York and work something out with Lacey."

"It's been weeks. She's probably moved on."

Josh hands me his phone.

"No, she hasn't. Far from it." I almost drop his phone because the voice came from it, not him.

I flip it over. *Sky?* I shoot a confused look to Josh. The last person I expected to see on the screen was her. I didn't even know they'd kept in touch. He hasn't mentioned her once since they left. *Partners in crime.*

"Hi, Sky. What do you mean?"

"By any chance have you spoken to your sister?"

"Chloe? She's called me twice, but I haven't called her back. Why? How do you know Chloe?"

"All I can say is that we need a plan. Josh and I are tired of the fucking bullshit we're dealing with on both sides. You need to get your sister on the phone, too, but I don't have much time. I offered to make a wine run so I could call Josh on the sly."

Right now, the only emotion I feel is hope.

24

LACEY

I've been floating on air since Monday. After I had the heart-to-heart with the girls, all of a sudden, I got a message from Will. It was a picture of the heart shell I left him the day I flew back. I'd left it by his phone on the boat. I wanted to call him right away, but I decided to play along. I sent him a picture of the Yankees hoodie I was wearing when we first met. I circled the tomato juice stain that hasn't come out, no matter how hard I've tried.

So then he responded with a picture of the dock where I fell into the water. I couldn't stop laughing. Me at my most graceful… not! We've continued this nonverbal communication right up until yesterday, but I didn't get anything else after I sent him a picture from *Baywatch*.

Until this morning, when he sent me a picture of a golden lasso. I practically jumped out of my skin from excitement. I've had a perma-grin on my face all day.

Work has been hectic this week, but Jocelyn gave everyone the afternoon off because Sophia and Sky are coming to the office in a few minutes. Sophia's asked Jocelyn to make her wedding dress. She hasn't designed wedding gowns before, but she immediately said yes. So now we're going to have a girls' afternoon here, sifting through fabrics, coming up with designs, and drinking a lot of wine and champagne. I'm glad they're including Sky in these things.

I tap my lips as I check to see if everything is set up in the sewing room. Chairs surround a large table that's next to Jocelyn's prepared sketching table. A mannequin stands nearby, ready and waiting for the party to begin. Yep, we're good.

The bell rings, alerting us that Sophia and Sky are here. Jocelyn beats me to the door and lets them in. She hugs them and whispers something in their ears. They giggle, then stop when they see me.

"Hey, Lace. Is the bubbly ready?" Sky approaches me with a goofy grin on her face.

"You're chipper today. I guess your boss got the space she wanted for the art studio?"

She looks at me like she has no idea what I'm talking about. "Huh? Oh! Yes." She needs something to drink.

We all stand around in the sewing room talking for a few minutes while Sky makes a phone call. I pop open the champagne bottle and get ready to pour.

The bell rings again. I glance at Jocelyn. "Are you expecting anyone?"

"No, but maybe it's a delivery. I'll go check, then we can get this party started."

A few minutes pass while Sophia chats about her family in Germany, and how happy her parents and sister are that the wedding will be held in the US.

What is taking Jocelyn so long?

I hear shuffling behind me and turn around. A woman stands there with a huge vase full of gorgeous pink peonies. "Are you Lacey Devlin?" she asks.

I nod because I think I'm about to swallow my tongue.

"Delivery for you."

She extends her arms to hand me the vase, but I'm frozen. Sophia thanks her and takes it for me. Then, like I need another shock, one after another, several more people come in, each carrying a vase full of peonies. They place them on every empty space they can find in this room. The scent already permeates the air.

The ringer on my phone startles me. I glance at it quickly to see who it is, and I do a double take. "Will?" My hands begin to sweat, and my heart is in my throat. I'm going to pass out. *He did this!* I'm so nervous, I don't know if I can answer. My hand hovers over the phone while yet another person comes in with another vase. There must be at least ten in here by now.

"No! No!" I shout at my phone when it stops ringing. I shake it and tap the screen. It starts ringing again, and I almost drop it. This is not the time to break it.

Tears prick my eyes because I'm so overwhelmed. Jocelyn and Sky stand in the doorway.

"What's the matter?" Jocelyn asks.

"I think it's Will." Sophia points to the phone and steps away.

"It's a video call," I say. "I'm freaking out."

"Well, answer it, dummy. This isn't the time to play chicken shit," Sky urges.

They're all standing there, looking at me and nodding.

They're right. I roll my shoulders, turn around, and lean my butt on the edge of the table. I tap the button. His face comes on the screen, and I cover my mouth. He's so gorgeous.

"Will, I can't believe it. It's so good to see you. I've missed you so much. And I'm so glad you called." I'm shaking and sweating profusely. "Did you do this?"

"Do what?" he says with a sexy smirk.

"You know what I mean. This." I turn my phone toward one of the vases, then turn it back to me.

"Maybe."

Huh? I look closer at the screen as he moves around. The walls in the background look familiar, and so does the painting on the wall. "W—wait a second. Will, where are you?"

"Right behind you."

I gasp and cover my mouth again. Tears start to spill, and I whirl around. I drop the phone on the table. *He's here!* In the flesh, and the only thing separating us is this damn table full of flowers.

"Hi, Red," he says softly.

I run around the table and jump on him. I wrap my legs around his waist as he lifts me up and squeezes me tight against him. We kiss as if it's the only thing that will save our lives. In a way it is. *Oh, how I've missed his lips.*

I finally break away from his yummy lips so I can breathe. I look over his shoulder and see several sets of eyes watching us. Jocelyn, Sophia, Sky, my brothers, Drew and Christian… and Will's sister, Chloe. *Really?*

Sky's holding her phone up with the screen facing us. I think I see Josh's face.

"We have an audience." I slide down his body and wrap my hands around his. "Guys, this is Will. But I guess you all know that already." Laughter fills the room.

"I can't believe you did this for me… for us? I'm so shocked. Thank you so much." I squeeze his side. I want to attack him again and push him on the table. Then I stop. "Wait. It's only May. You said you don't come back until July."

"We have some partners in crime who helped work this out. It seems a lot of people are on our side, and they made it happen so I could come earlier." He glances at Sky and then Chloe. Then waves to Sky's phone. "Right, Josh and Sawyer?" *Wow, Sawyer too.*

I take the phone out of Sky's hand.

"You bet," Josh says. "He's been a miserable bastard since you left. Someone had to take charge."

Another guy appears on the screen. I chuckle

because his face is so close to the phone. "I'm Sawyer. Take care of him. He's the best guy I know."

"Hi, Sawyer. Will *is* the best… and the cutest too." He grins.

Will takes the phone out of my hand and gives it back to Sky. Then he stands in front of me.

"So, I need to ask you something."

My eyes bulge. My heart rate speeds up to the point I might need to go to the hospital. My heart has gotten more exercise since I met him than it had the whole last year.

"Someone told me you might be looking for a new job. Maybe one that entails a lot of sun and sand."

I peek around him and see Sky grinning behind her hand. I giggle, then focus on him again.

"We have some openings at our marinas. The only requirement is that you have to wear that red bathing suit to clinch the deal. The job starts immediately. Interested?"

A surge of excitement lights me up like a Christmas tree. "I'll wear anything you want every second of every day if it means I get to spend the rest of my life with you."

He rubs my arms. "I know this is a leap of faith and we have a lot to discuss. But from the very first time I saw you, my heart was right. You're the only one for me, Lace. Take this leap with me."

I grip his shirt in my hands and raise up on my toes. "Yes! I'm so in love with you, and it feels so good to say it out loud. It's been torture without you."

He cups my face. "I love you too, and I promise

you'll never regret choosing us." His hand covers my heart. "You know that lasso around your heart that's connected to mine?"

I nod.

"It's permanent." Our bodies inch closer together.

"I guess that means you're stuck with me then."

He caresses my lips with his. "Forever."

The End

I hope you enjoyed Lacey and Will's love story. Colors and Curves is next with Skylar and Julius's story. Don't miss out.

ALSO BY KRISTINA BECK

Collide Series

Lives Collide

Dreams Collide

Souls Collide

Collide Series Box Set

Four Seasons Series

Snowflakes and Sapphires - Winter

Passions and Peonies - Spring

Colors and Curves - Summer

Maple Trees and Maybes - Autumn

Standalone Novels

Into Thin Air

Love Ever After Anthology

ACKNOWLEDGMENTS

Around twenty years ago, I cruised around the British Virgin Islands in a motorboat with family and friends. We lived in our bathing suits the entire time and didn't have a care in the world. The scenery was breath-taking and the atmosphere forced me to relax and have fun. Until this day, it is still my favorite vacation.

When Lacey's character came along, I knew she'd be the perfect fit for this plot and location. I'm happy that I could finally use my experience in one of my books. It brought back so many memories. Because this is a novella, I couldn't go into as much detail as I wanted.

It was my sister, Deanna's, honeymoon that we celebrated on this trip. The newlyweds arrived a couple of days before us and then we took off with the boat for a week. Deanna and her husband, Gene, have years of experience with motorboats. They assisted me with the technical terms and facts about driving them. Thank you for your help!

My husband and kids are the best. They keep me sane when I'm writing like a mad woman. When I doubt my abilities, they always reassure me that I can do anything. Shouldn't I be doing that for them? Anyway, I love them to bits and I know I'm a very blessed wife and mother. Ich liebe euch!

It's time to thank the many people I'm surrounded by during my writing process. To my beta readers, Ilona Ahrens, Jamie Buck, and Rachel Childers, thank you for your support and friendship. You always strive to help me improve my stories. I appreciate you taking the time out of your busy schedules to read this book over and over again. You're all amazing.

I can't emphasize enough how much I love this book cover. Jody Kaye, you created one that made my eyes tear the first time I saw it. That has never happened before and you know that I love all of my covers. Thank you for agreeing to create the covers for the entire Four Seasons Series. It's an honor and I can't wait to see what we come up with for the next books in the series.

To my editing team, Rachel Overton and Helen Pryke, because of you, my books are of the highest quality when they're finished. I don't trust my books with anyone else. Thank you for your keen eye for detail, encouragement, and love for my books. I hope we have a long future together in the writing business.

Thank you, Rik Hall, for your endless dependability, great formatting, and quick turnaround. I don't know what I'd do without you.

And to my devoted readers, I'd never be at this point if it weren't for you. When I wrote my first book, I couldn't imagine writing five more in so little time. Your never-ending praise, friendship, laughter, and encouragement pushes me to become a better writer and to never stop. I'll never be able to fully express my appreciation of you. Social media doesn't do it justice. Maybe one day, I will be able to meet all of you. Thank you for everything!

ABOUT THE AUTHOR

Kristina Beck was born and raised in New Jersey, USA, and lived there for thirty years. She later moved to Germany and now lives there with her German husband and three children. She is an avid reader of many genres, but romance always takes precedence. She loves coffee, dark chocolate, power naps, flowers, and eighties movies. Her hobbies include writing, reading, fitness, and forever trying to improve her German-language skills.

For more updates on her books, sign up for her newsletter and follow her on social media.
www.kristinabeck.com

facebook.com/krissybeck73

instagram.com/krissybeck96

amazon.com/author/kristinabeck

bookbub.com/authors/kristina-beck

goodreads.com/kristina_beck

Printed in Great Britain
by Amazon

67536903R00113